HEROES AND IDOLS

Richard Baran

Mouse Gate™ Adventures
1103 Middlecreek
Friendswood, Texas 77546
281-992-3131   281-482-5390 Fax
www.mousegate.com

ISBN: 978-1-59095-318-1
UPC: 6-43977-43185-1
Library of Congress Control Number: 2015954556

Printed in the United States of America with simultaneous printings in
Australia, Canada, and United Kingdom.

FIRST EDITION
1   2   3   4   5   6   7   8   9   10

A. M. D. G.

Author Richard Baran

holds a doctorate and two masters' degrees besides his bachelor's in business. A Navy veteran, he taught and coached for forty years at the secondary school and collegiate levels. His publishing credits include, a coaching text, *Coaching Football's Polypotent Offense* a short story, *That Ain't No Walleye*, and several dozen articles in professional journals.

Baran's first novel, *The Jacket,* was published by Total Recall Press as were his subsequent novels, *Where Have All The Go-Go's Gone? Part One; When Will They Ever Learn—Where Have All The Go-Go's Gone? Part Two, Shutter Bug, Heroes and Idles, Did You Boo Hopalong Cassidy.*and *The Dutchman's Gift.*

Dick and his eighth grade sweetheart, Carol, have eighteen grandchildren and they divide their year between Franklin Park, Illinois; Phoenix, Arizona and Minocqua, Wisconsin.

Visit www.richardbaran.com for more information.

About The Book

A burlesque star, an Ojibwa Indian Chief, three cantankerous grandfathers--one a Prussian officer from World War I--an immigrant Italian grandmother who drank straight whiskey from a Mason jar and a Chicago Cub baseball hero change four young lives forever.

Tess, Stan, Georgie and Gil had their *Heroes and Idols*. Tess worshipped her World War II era burlesque star, Aunt Rose and Chief John Proud Bear in *Lunch with a Gypsy*. Georgie, a young father entangled in an affair, drew guidance from his immigrant Italian grandmother, Nana Beam's whiskey induced lessons about repentance in *I've Got a Secret*. Stan idolized his two grandfathers, Grampa Zev and Gramps and lessons he learned from them along with a big fish, class ring and a heart he had inscribed in an old maple tree when he reconnected with El B, his high school sweetheart from forty years ago in *The One Who Got Away*. Gil struggled to comprehend why his baseball idol had been traded and why his father had died as he was just getting to know him in *Trading Prushka*.

PART I
Lunch with a Gypsy

Chapter 1

It didn't look like a potato, but that's how her aunt explained it to her. "You're looking at Potato Lake, Precious," said Aunt Rose, her voice box appearing to be lined in coarse grit sandpaper; one hand on Tess's shoulder, the other moving slowly from left to right tracing the dense, wooded shoreline. The raspy sounds of the explanation that rattled from her throat resembled lumps of brown sugar combined with too many Pall Malls and glasses of Cutty Sark and in no way matched up with the slender graceful hands of a burlesque star.

"It doesn't look like any potato I've ever seen," said Tess, her cheek brushing against the top of her aunt's comforting hand.

Aunt Rose, the twinkle in her eyes hidden behind the Army Air Corps style sun glasses she wore, gave a gentle brush to Tess's cheek with her fingers. "It's only a name, Precious."

Aunt Rose, who really wasn't her aunt, was a second or third cousin to her mother, if that close. She was the only one who had or ever would call Tess, Precious. To everyone else the seven year old girl with the shoulder length, brown pig-tails was Tess or Little Tess.

Tess had heard from listening to adults, her relatives and a few of her parent's friends that Auntie Rose, as she called her, was a dancer; her curiosity taking her no further. She was in awe of her aunt, Tess being dwarfed by who she thought was a beautiful slender giant with eyes the color of Potato Lake; eyes that seemed to protect her with a gentle caress. Tess always thought that her Aunt Rose had the most amazing walk, flowing like a gentle breeze when she moved, her auburn hair drifting along, fluttering with the current. Aunt Rose did more than flow when she danced. Her chosen profession was burlesque and what Tess didn't know was that Aunt Rose was world famous. She didn't look world famous with her hair now pulled back, lips minus applied color and her ever present cigarette holder protruding from her mouth. Aunt Rose wanted no part of fame. What she wanted was her one true love in life and that was the reason she was in northern Wisconsin in the small town of Hayward. Aunt Rose loved to fish. More specifically, Aunt Rose loved to fish for Musky. It was her passion.

Tess stood next to her aunt on Potato Lake's sandy shore looking puzzled and wondering why a lake would be named after a vegetable. Most of the potatoes she had seen were mashed because that's what her father and two older brothers, Buzz and Donny seem to consume by grotesque mouthfuls, barnyard sounds escaping from their mouths. What she really loved, however, was the aroma of her mother's potato pancakes. They had a special smell that made her nose pucker creating tiny creases. It didn't matter that they were recycled mashed potatoes combined with a liberal amount of grated onion, some flour, an egg and then pummeled extra thin with her mother's hands. She didn't need to close her eyes to see those pancakes frying in spattering lard. Eating them didn't appeal to her as much as the exotic smell emanating from the enormous cast iron skillet that made her drool. Anticipation made her tiny nose continue to twitch with pleasure like a contented cat during the entire preparation as she stood behind her mother at the chipped, white enamel gas stove.

The sight of Potato Lake was an overpowering, almost eerie, sight to the seven year old. It wasn't the size. Potato Lake was like her tiny fish bowl at home compared to Lake Michigan where she had gone several times with her mother to the Foster Avenue Beach. Potato Lake didn't have her pet tetra, Baby and Ruth either. On each of her trips to the Foster Avenue Beach with her mother, she found herself enthralled by the sight of sailboats gliding across the choppy water of Lake Michigan. She would stand with her slightly pigeon toed feet buried in the grainy sand of the Chicago beach mesmerized by the billowing white sails, some with rainbow stripes, like puffed out chests of a parade of drum majors strutting and leading a parade. There were no white sails dotting Potato Lake, just the green and emerging white pods of lily pads appearing to float on the calm surface. What intrigued Tess most were the trees surrounding the shore of the lake; their thick curtain of shades of green preventing her from seeing into the woods; making her wonder what surprises were being hidden from her; perhaps the wild Indians her brother Donny had warned her about saying in a whisper: "Them Injuns just might chop off your pigtails with their Tommyhawks." Donny ended his hushed warning with a loud, "Boo!" as he reached out and pretended to grab her.

Tess had never seen so many trees in one place in her short life except in a forest preserve where her parents once took her and her brothers to a family reunion picnic. She never forgot putting a wiener on a whittled tree branch her father had sharpened for her then watching as if in a trance as the wiener began to sizzle and smoke. That was before the war came and before her father and her oldest brother, Buzz weren't at home anymore.

"But, Auntie Rose," she asked, standing next to her aunt on the shore, her worn, brown scuffed oxfords half buried in the sand, "why are some of the trees straight and the others all crooked and messy?"

Her aunt slid her hand from Tess's shoulder and gently stroked the little girl's hair, her right hand now holding the pearl cigarette holder with the ever smoldering Pall Mall. "Precious," she said, her eyes scanning the perimeter of the lake, adoring every inch, "those are the three choices Mother Nature gives to everyone: Straight, crooked, or messy." Then, without looking down at the questioning eyes, her hand still stroking the silken hair, she added, "Always be thankful that you're straight like those bull rushes." She nodded towards the tall reeds interspersed among the lily pads and being caressed by what her aunt referred to as, "Musky cabbage" that lined the shore of the lake leisurely weaving through the lily pads as if lost in a seductive dance. "When the wind blows hard those reeds bend, but they never break." The palm of Aunt Rose's hand rested gently on top of Tess's head. "Precious, as you get older and go through life you might encounter a wind that blows hard," she said, her hand giving a loving stroke to Tess's pigtails. "Never forget those bull rushes."

* * * * *

Years later, after Aunt Rose had made her final curtain call and Tess had raised two daughters of her own; she never forgot the bull rushes and Mother Nature's choices. Memories of the trees surrounding Potato Lake were etched into her mind; vivid portraits; the colors of tree trunks flashing white and black or beige and chocolate brown, dark moss stained bark on some. The jagged shapes of different green leaves and pointed needles of pines still reflected off the mirror finish of the tranquil lake resting contented in her mind. She never forgot her aunt's message about standing up straight, bending, but never breaking. The trees and the rushes were a sight she wanted her daughters to experience, but they had always balked when she brought up the idea of a vacation. Her husband, too, joined his daughters' negative replies for a Northwoods vacation. His real balking would come later in private; his displeasure consisting of punctuation marks made with slaps and fists, sometimes kicks. She accepted her daughters' excuses, covering her disappointment while applying heavy make-up to her bruises; the ones that were visible. She knew her Aunt Rose, and even her mother, would have answered their excuses with a glare that would have sent both girls packing for the Northwoods. The glare was a technique she should have used when raising her girls, but she was too busy defending herself from a constant barrage of other glares and the blowing and howling of fierce ugly winds that tried to break her.

Chapter 2

Tess still could recall how sorry she felt for some of the trees; those that had fallen along the shoreline of Potato Lake; some twisted and barren of leaves their branches reaching out like fallen warriors grasping for their Happy Hunting Ground and eternal peace. Some of the trees lay in the water on twisted angles, the messy option of Mother Nature. "Why is there a funny looking big chunk missing from that poor tree," she asked her aunt.

"Have you ever heard of the expression, busy beaver," her aunt replied.

Tess nodded, wide eyed. "Beavers?" she asked, then adding an almost frightened, "Really?"

"Sometime the saw-like teeth of a busy beaver will make a tree fall down," her aunt continued.

"Really," Tess asked again? Her questions spilled out non-stop; her mother's warning about being a pest forgotten.

Potato Lake sat like a color photograph mounted on one of the black pages in her mother's family album that rested on an end table in the living room of their tiny house. The hypnotic lake now became Tess's personal come-to-life photo album minus the actual pages and photographs yet stirring up question after question. "Auntie, why did you call those things with the dark ends sticking out of the water bull rushes?"

"That's what God called them in the Bible, Precious."

"But I think they look like what my grandma makes me for

breakfast when I stay by her when my mommy and daddy go away for a weekend."

"You're grandmother makes you reeds for breakfast?"

She could see the smile on her aunt's lips, the sunglasses hiding the twinkle. "No," she said starting to giggle. "Grandma makes me pigs-in-a-blanket."

"They may look like your grandmother's pigs-in-a-blanket, but they're bull rushes to your Aunt Rose," said her aunt. "And those darned Musky love to wrap my line around them."

"Musky, Aunt Rose?"

"That's right, Precious," replied her aunt, a serious tone being added to her voice as she added, "A Musky."

She watched her aunt push her sunglasses above her eyes to her forehead and saw a strange look on her aunt's face as a swirl of her cigarette smoke was carried away by a gentle breath of wind. "What's a Musky?" asked Tess sounding both curious and afraid.

There was a raspy laugh. "A Musky is a fish," said Aunt Rose, converting her laugh to a slight smile. "It's a fierce fish, Precious; A fish that can be beautiful yet a brute; a fish that can grow to be as big as you and even bigger."

Tess took several steps back from the lake. "Are there any Musky in there?" she asked, her finger pointing cautiously toward the water.

"Precious, I sure as hell hope so," said Aunt Rose, the grit of her sandpaper voice growing coarser.

Tess suddenly wished she were staying with her grand-mother in Chicago. There she would be safe and secure in the old brownstone on Walton Street, eating pigs-in-a-blanket instead of being far from her mother and the security of the tiny frame Salt Box crying for paint and the leaning front porch she knew as home. Central and Drummond streets were home, not Hayward, Wisconsin. "Auntie Rose," she said timidly, now remembering her mother's warnings about being a pest, "Why did we have to go so far away from home for a vacation?"

"Precious," her aunt said, burying her cigarette butt in the sandy beach with her fishing boot while her slim delicate fingers dug out another Pall Mall from the package stuck in the breast pocket of her black and red checked wool lumberjack shirt. "It's not going far away. It's going to..." She paused, reaching out to stroke Tess's hair again.... "Everyone needs a very special place to go to."

"Like my brother, Donny, and his friend, Shorty, who go to their hiding place they dug in the ground in the vacant lot on the corner near our house?"

"That is indeed a special place."

"So why did we come so far to be with some old monster Musky?"

Aunt Rose gently lowered her hand from Tess's hair and placed it around her shoulder. "Look around, Precious. Look around at this special place," she said pausing as if lost in her thoughts. "I'd wander the world over like a gypsy looking for a place like this."

"What's a gypsy, Auntie," Tess asked looking up at her statuesque, almost enchanting, aunt.

"A gypsy, Precious is a person who doesn't stay in one spot too long," replied her aunt with a smile. "I'm kind of like a gypsy; my job, if you can call it that, doesn't allow me to stay in one spot too long."

Tess thought she understood, but too many questions were

pushing and shoving at one another to get out of her mouth with special leading the way. Her eyes continued tracing the shoreline, not sure of what she was supposed to look for, then glancing up at her aunt. "I guess special means straight, crooked, and messy like all of those trees."

Her aunt knelt down on one knee in the sand looking into Tess's questioning eyes, her own eyes turning sad. "Don't you think your father would like to be here on vacation instead of where he's at now?" she asked, as other family members' names followed. "And wouldn't your mother like being here with you right now?" Aunt Rose continued to ask in a soothing voice. "And Buzz?" she continued. "Even Donny instead of in his hiding place? All of you would be together." Her head nodded toward the lake. "I know I'm happy to be here with you and not stuck somewhere with the crooked and messy."

"I'm happy to be here with you too, Auntie," replied Tess, knowing that being with her family on another picnic or, better yet, a vacation was her secret dream instead of having her mother and father dropping her off when they went away while Buzz looked out after Donny at home. Her mother and father weren't on vacation now. Her dad and Buzz were off fighting in a war. Her dad was drafted into the army, but Buzz, who celebrated his eighteenth birthday by dropping out of Lane Tech High School a month before graduation, enlisted in the navy. At first, everyone thought the Army made a mistake when Tess's father had been drafted. "He's too old," she remembered hearing, along with, "The guys got three kids." None of that made sense to her. What she tried to understand was that both her father and brother were in faraway places she had never heard of and that her mother cried a lot. Now she was in her own faraway place, on vacation; her very first one and with her favorite aunt. "Am I a gypsy, Auntie Rose?"

Chapter 3

Tess was apprehensive at first when she first saw her aunt pull up to the house with two men in a black Cadillac. The two men were, as she learned, Aunt Rose's agent, Mr. Sid, and her choreographer, Mr. Joe. Tess saw Mr. Sid as a much older version of her brother, Buzz. Mr. Sid's wavy black hair was as wavy as Buzz's, the part running almost down the middle of his head, but the natural wave was thinner and lighter like a wave that had expended itself on the shore of Lake Michigan. Where he differed from her brother was in the way his head and hands seemed to be coordinated in a continuous agitated dancing motion that made Tess nervous. She did like his smile even though it was bigger than Buzz's. What she didn't like was seeing a mouth full of once perfect teeth that were stained an ugly brown.

Mr. Curly made Tess laugh the moment she saw him emerge from the passenger side of the shiny Cadillac. Tess had no idea what a choreographer was, but she did like the former burlesque comic who still wore baggy pants and insisted that she call him Curly even though he was bald. She had respectfully addressed them, as her mother had instructed, from their first meeting until the vacation ended as Mr. Sid and Mr. Curly. Aunt Rose called the men her cronies and usually addressed them as one with expressions that were more like a warning to unruly children: "Will you two stop it!" was her most use admonition.

It bothered Tess at first that it just wasn't she and her aunt going on a vacation like her mother had explained to her. Her apprehension quickly turned to an attraction for the two men who, from the onset of the special vacation, hovered around Tess like a pair of knights in shining armor. There were a stack of comic books waiting for her in the back seat of the Cadillac; her eyes as big as the comic books' colored covers, wanting to touch them but not daring. Before the car was a block away from Tess's house the first candy bar, a Hershey, was being passed back from the front seat. Her eyes almost popped out.

"Is that for me?" she asked, ignoring the laughter that followed her question. She didn't understand why her aunt had said to Mr. Sid and Mr. Curly, "Will you two characters stop acting like a couple of kids and grow up." Tess didn't care.

Tess cared even less when they stopped for lunch and she ate the biggest hamburger she had even seen and washed it down with an even bigger milk shake that had a swirl of whipped cream on top and a maraschino cherry. She had never even seen a maraschino cherry before.

All of Tess's cares left once they arrived at their destination in a place called Hayward. "It's in Wisconsin," her mother had tried to explain to her.

For Tess, Wisconsin could have been on the Moon once her Aunt Rose's cronies began buying her all the Coca Cola in the curved glass bottles she wanted. Radio Joe's, the resort where they stayed could have been on Mars. Tess didn't care. She would sit at the polished, dark hardwood bar in the dining room of Radio Joe's Resort with her aunt, Mr. Sid and Mr. Curly before dinner, a Coca Cola bottle in front of her, swiveling on the bar stool with the chrome legs, going back and forth until she felt her aunt's gentle touch on her knee. The two men would take turns slipping her a candy bar, both ignoring her aunt's admonishments because too much chocolate wasn't good for a little girl; her exact words: "Don't you two guys know there's a war on and chocolate's a scarcity?" There was sip of her scotch as she referred to it as, "On the rock" because of the single cube in her glass; one of her aunt's many idiosyncrasies. "You two characters are going to fill her up on sweet stuff and ruin her appetite for dinner."

Sid and Curly sloughed off the admonishment as did Radio Joe the proprietor who seemed to have a never ending supply of candy.

Tess always thanked them for the treats, ever polite, extending her hand to Mr. Sid, Mr. Curly or Mr. Radio as she respectfully referred to each. She had heard her father tell her brothers that they should always use the word, Mister in front of an adult male's name when addressing him; Mam to adult women. Tess also tried not to be a pest and remembered what her mother had told her about washing her hands and keeping her nails clean. "If you don't, worms will build a home under them," her mother had said to her while filling up the tub in their lone bathroom on Saturday night. Being the youngest, she got to use the bath water first, her mother last.

Chapter 4

Tess still couldn't believe she was standing next to her aunt in a strange, faraway place called Wisconsin looking at a lake named after a potato. What frightened her was that another man had joined her aunt and the cronies. She wasn't expecting someone who she might have to share her Hershey bar and Cokes with; not someone with black hair streaked with grey, the hair in a single braid stopping at his shoulder blades. He didn't look like any other man she had ever seen. Tess was fascinated by the color of his skin. It was darker than hers and she couldn't get over his face. She thought she was looking at the picture on a nickel she kept in her tiny, pink piggy bank, the pig's eyes set off with long, curly painted black lashes. His name, she later learned, was Chief John Proud Bear. Her Aunt Rose called him Chief John and he was to be their fishing guide. Tess didn't fully comprehend what a guide was but she understood that he was a real Indian; an Ojibwa who, along with the cronies, bull rushes, Mother Nature's choices and Musky were many of the new snap shots quickly filling the photo album in her mind.

Tess liked most of the photographs in her new album that was showing traces of starting to bulge. She didn't like, however, the white frame cottage with the chipped, faded and stained white paint and the porch with its loose screens that waved and flapped in the slightest breeze. "Nothing but the best for you, Rose," she heard Radio Joe tell her aunt when showing her where she and her niece would sleep. She shared a big bed with her aunt; the sagging mattress letting out a low, groaning squeak the moment weight of any kind trespassed on it. Tess felt like she was lying on a giant bag mixed with equal parts marbles and marshmallows. What she disliked even more was that her aunt would tuck her and Patsy, her pillowcase doll with the button eyes and nose, under the covers in the musty smelling bed saying, "Now you and Pasty get some sleep. We have a big day tomorrow with those Musky."

"Auntie Rose," asked Tess, the first time her aunt had tucked her in. "Where are you going?"

"To check with Mr. Radio about what time our guide, Chief John will be here tomorrow to take us fishing," replied her aunt. She gave the blanket another tug and kissed Tess on the forehead. "Now you and Pasty get some sleep."

"But, Aunt...."

"Ssshhhhhh," said Aunt Rose, her index finger gently brushing Tess's lips. "I'll be right back."

"But, Auntie Rose," Tess blurted out, while trying to be polite, "my doll's name is Patsy, not Pasty."

Her aunt smiled, took a sophisticated puff of her cigarette jutting out from the pearl holder and apologized. "I'm sorry, Precious. I get work and your doll's name all mixed up." She gave yet another tuck on the covers and kissed her cheek. "Now sleep tight and don't let the bed bugs bite."

She knew her aunt was only joking about the bed bugs, and she would be close by in the lodge's bar with her cronies. It was the sound of the Namagakon River flowing by some twenty yards down a rocky hill from her bedroom window that scared her, making her cling to her doll, saying: "Don't worry, Patsy,

I'll take care of you if any of those Musky monsters sneak out of the river and try to get us."

Even though the noise of the river and the musty smell of the cabin frightened her at night, she was still intrigued by the resort's name. When she first learned she was going on a vacation with her Aunt Rose she had no idea what or where a Radio Joe was. She was too afraid to ask and too curious not to after she heard her aunt say to her mother, "We'll be spending a full week up north in Hayward. The place is called Radio Joe's and it comes highly recommended. Good Musky fishing," is what her aunt had explained. Both her aunt and mother laughed when Tess had asked, "Does this Mister Joe person look like the radio we have in our living room?"

Several more of her questions brought her mother's warning about not being a pest. Even in the car her curiosity shoved aside those warnings. "What's a Hayward?" she asked.

"You'll see," her aunt said where they both sat in the Cadillac's spacious back seat. There was a reassuring pat on Tess's knee and then her Aunt Rose would appear to lose patience with her two cronies.

Tess could hear Mr. Sid muttering to Mr. Curly in the front seat of the Cadillac about something called an Army convoy and Camp McCoy and using words that Tess knew were bad. She overheard her mother tell Donny once, after hearing him shout at his neighbor friend, Shorty, calling him, "You fuckin' Kraut," that she'd not only wash his mouth out with Lava soap, but slap him silly first if he ever used vile language like that again. Then she heard her Aunt Rose ask Mr. Curly, "Jesus Christ, are you trying to get us killed?"

Mr. Curly was driving on the wrong side of the two lane

road, honking the Cadillac's horn as he passed truck after truck of the Army convoy heading for Camp McCoy. Curly had replied to Aunt Rose, using what Tess thought was God's name, that it would take them two hours longer to get to Hayward if he had to follow the trucks. Then Tess heard Mr. Sid reply in what resembled a curse and a shriek, "You got the goddamn speedometer needle buried, you moron." Then she saw her aunt lean forward, her hands sliding around Mr. Curly's neck. "Getting us there dead isn't going to do any of us any good," said her aunt. Then Tess dove for the corner of the back seat when she heard her aunt shout: "Slow down you son of a bitch!"

Tess didn't know if Mr. Curly slowed down. All she could see out of the side window where her aunt had retreated was canvas covered truck after canvas covered truck being passed and waving hands extended out the back of each truck. Then she felt her aunt's gentle touch on her shoulder. "We'll be just fine," she heard her aunt say.

Chapter 5

Her Aunt Rose's description of Radio Joe's had been right. It was also overwhelming and frightening to Tess. She looked up in awe almost tipping over backwards at the biggest and only radio tower she had ever seen. The silver metal grid next to the resort's dark stained log lodge poked its way heavenward beyond the tops of the pines. She stood next to her aunt, latched onto her hand, her eyes dancing back and forth from the tower to the strange looking little man with the continuous nervous laugh who had greeted them as they drove up.

"When the weather's right, I can get the war news from Europe," the man named Radio Joe told her aunt. Then lowering his voice for fear of bruising tender ears, "I can even get the GI's cheering and whistling for you."

"I'm on vacation, Joe," her Aunt Rose said, slapping him on the back. "The only cheering I want to hear is when I get my Musky."

Radio Joe wore glasses, the lens on one side cracked and the wire temple on the other side held in place with a tiny safety pin and covered with black electrician's tape. His brown wing tip shoes were minus the laces and appeared to not have seen polish since before the war. He was short with grey hair badly in need of a trim and had, what Tess had never seen, hair growing from his ears. "Rose," he said, his voice still lowered, "the Musky will chew each others' tails off trying to get at your buck tail." Tess saw the wink from behind the cracked lens.

Aunt Rose grinned, slapped Radio Joe on the back again and then kept her arm draped around his shoulders. "Any chance of hearing anything tonight?" she asked seriously. "My cousin's husband is in Europe, and the kid's older brother is somewhere in the Pacific."

"I've got an uncle fighting in Europe," said Curly meekly.

"I've got relatives in Poland we haven't heard from since the war broke out," added Mr. Sid.

"My brother, Donny, says that Buzz is on a Tin Can," Tess quickly spurted out as four sets of eyes stayed serious.

Radio Joe knelt down on one knee and said to Tess, his voice filled with compassion and understanding even though his breath was not, "I'll see what I can find out about your brother and father."

"Thank you, Mr. Radio," Tess said, her nose rebelling at the smell of tobacco coating over what she recalled was the foul aroma of their basement in Chicago after a heavy rain made the sewer water back up.

From the very beginning, Tess looked forward to seeing Mr. Radio each day. When she went to the lodge with her aunt for breakfast and dinner with Mr. Sid and Mr. Curly Mr. Radio had a treat for her. She never knew that potato chips came in tiny cellophane bags and that so much candy existed as Mr. Radio explained, "Sweets for the sweetest little girl ever to be served in my establishment."

Tess didn't know what an establishment was, but she could see her aunt beam when Mr. Radio added, "Rose, you are one lucky aunt and this little girl's parents are even luckier."

The compliments and the treats kept coming after breakfast

and dinner and didn't stop until her aunt took her back to the cabin to tuck her in for the night. From the time her aunt pulled the crisp white sheet and the torn goose down comforter up to Tess's neck until Tess fell asleep, she clutched onto Patsy. She comforted her doll, telling her not to be afraid of the spooky shadows of the trees reaching out to the cabin in the eerie moonlight. Patsy, her button eyes big and wide coming off a hand-me-down winter coat that Tess had outgrown, seemed to understand what her protector was saying. They were both going to be safe from what appeared to be more than the sound of the Namakagon River whooshing and gurgling as it bounced over rocks barely sticking out of the water. Trying to stay brave, she would say to Patsy, "Auntie Rose says there might be a Musky for me to catch." Then, pulling her doll closer to her as she burrowed under the covers, "I don't know if I want to catch some mean old monster," she confessed. "But, you know what, Patsy?" she added. "Mr. Radio will scare all the old monsters away and then give us both a treat." Tess let out a sigh. "If only his breath wasn't like p.u. stinky."

After several nights, Tess had made friends with the darkness, cuddled with the lumps in the mattress and decided she liked the musty smell of the cottage. She didn't mind the dining room filled with cigarette smoke because Mr. Sid and Mr. Curly were always surprising her with treats. On her second night there, Mr. Curly made her giggle by telling her to close her eyes and stick out her hands. He had placed a Baby Ruth in each hand and said, "I didn't want you to get lonely for your two gold fish." She thanked him with a big smile and added, "They're tetra, Mr. Curly." Her Aunt Rose, left hand holding the pearl cigarette holder and the right clutching an on-the-rocks glass of Cutty Sark, her one rock a single ice chip, slammed the glass down on the table so hard everything jumped including Tess, Mr. Curly and Mr. Sid. "Jesus Christ," shouted her jubilant aunt. "You are precious!"

Tess didn't feel precious on the next night after dinner when she got her first taste of what she thought was a slice of rye bread covered with blackberry jam. Her aunt led her by the hand, the one without the Hershey Bar, to the bar to ask Radio Joe if he had heard any war news. "Nothing specific, Rose," said Joe business like. "The good news is we're winning in Europe and the Pacific." He looked empathetically at Tess who was seated on one of the swivel bar stools gazing at the mirror along the back bar. "I haven't heard anything about your daddy and brother." He paused. "But, believe me, you'll be the first to know if I do." He paused, gave Tess a wink and said, "And I'm betting it will be the best news ever."

Tess watched Radio Joe move toward the middle of the bar, pick up a plate filled with what looked like tiny slices of a dark bread and return, placing the plate down in front of her aunt. "A treat for you, Rose," he said. Reaching under the bar he brought out a small, open tin can and set it in front of her aunt. Then he slid a butter knife next to the plate.

"Caviar," Rose exclaimed with a smile. "And pumpernickel."

"Pumpernickel, Auntie?" Tess asked forgetting about being a pest.

"Rye bread, Precious," her aunt said without a trace of correcting. Her aunt looked pleased as she asked Radio Joe, "Do you treat all your guests this way?"

Radio Joe leaned forward. "Only my most famous and

classiest ones," he whispered.

Tess heard her aunt's coarse laugh but was more interested in the plate of bread and the open tin its jagged top bent back exposing what looked like blackberry jam. She had eaten rye bread at her grandmother's house, her grandmother's homemade blackberry jam spread so thick on it that it oozed over the sides making her fingers sticky. She couldn't take her eyes off the dark lumpy mixture in the tin. That's when Mr. Curly said to her after buying her a bottle of Coca Cola, "Go 'head, Precious, take a bite. It's from Russia."

"Excuse me, Mr. Curly," she said with defiant politeness and having no idea of what Russia meant. "My name is Tess and only my Auntie Rose can call me Precious."

"Sure, kid," Curly said pushing the saucer with the bread in her direction. "Your Auntie Rose loves this stuff."

Her aunt placed a tiny dab of caviar on the end of a piece of pumpernickel. "Take a taste to see if you like it."

Tess didn't hesitate. Blackberry jam was one of her favorites.

After they had all laughed at the expression on her face and the speed at which the top of the Coca Cola bottle found her tiny mouth; her aunt gave her a hug. "Precious," she said smiling, "one of these days you'll cultivate a taste for the finer things in life."

The yucky salty fish egg episode, as she would refer to it later in life, was on the night before the most memorable time of her Wisconsin vacation.

As she sat down for breakfast at her usual spot at the table with the red and white checked table cloth, Radio Joe stopped by and said to her, "I tried to find some news for you, but there wasn't any." He patted her on the shoulder. Then adding, "Don't worry, Tess, no news is always good." She knew that wasn't the case. Any news, no news, old news made her mother cry. And when her mother wasn't crying she was writing letters hoping and praying for news. And when she wasn't crying or writing she was collecting tin cans and newspapers. She saved every drop of bacon grease when there was any to save and tended her Victory Garden that covered half the small back yard of their house that stood in the triangle of streets she had learned made up her neighborhood called Logan Square. Everyone had a Victory Garden in her neighborhood. The Brzozowski's, their Polish neighbors, even raised chickens in their garage. After her father had gone off to war, Mr. Brzozowski would bring over eggs. His generosity lasted only a short time and stopped after her mother had said to him, "Don't you ever put your hand..." And that's all Tess remembered except Mr. Brzozowski leaving their gangway with what looked like a big yellow stain on his shirt.

As she and Patsy snuggled comfortably under the covers of the lumpy, sagging bed, she tried to imagine her father fighting the Germans. She had watched while her twelve-year-old brother, Donny, and his best friend, Shorty Schultz played a game they called, *Nip the Nips* each taking turns to be one of the dirty Nips, whoever they were. They never killed any imaginary Germans although there was the bad word incident between Donny and Shorty. She'd watch and listen to her brother and Shorty do imitations of Spike Jones giving the raspberries right in the Fuhrer's face. Tess tried to imitate her brother and Shorty in the privacy of the family's one bathroom, looking into the mirror, sticking out her tongue, blowing and then thinking at how messy it was. Donny wasn't as good as Shorty, who gave the juiciest of raspberries because he hated Hitler. So did his parents because Shorty's older brother, Michael, had been wounded in action during the Battle of the Bulge and was coming home minus one arm.

Chapter 6

Tess's imaginary photo album of her vacation kept getting bigger by the hour and was close to busting at the seams; the cover groaning with each opening and closing. Every day more pictures were etched onto the pages. It would have been a perfect vacation except for the caviar and the stream of men coming to their table during dinner to talk to her aunt. She liked the way Mr. Sid and Mr. Curly would protect her aunt. Mr. Sid would tell the men with a smile, "You'll get your autographs the night before we leave." Then giving each an exaggerated wink, "And we'll even throw in a picture for you." He'd give whoever had interrupted dinner a smile and say, "How's that?"

Most of the men were polite, dragging their feet as they left, never taking their eyes off her aunt. A few men seemed too persistent, and that's when Mr. Curly would quickly get up from his chair, the top of his bald head wrinkled as was his scowl and say, "Give her a break, pal. She's on vacation." Then Curly gave a sheepish pause and said, "I am too." That was followed by a sigh and Curly finishing with, "Taking a break from the pro wrestling circuit if you know what I mean."

That tactic usually worked because Mr. Curly could change his demeanor in an instant, the result of his vaudeville experiences and also several years as a professional wrestler when he was a young man. He had whispered to Tess saying, "I was about the age of your brother, Buzz when I wrestled."

She thought that none of the men who stopped by the table to talk with her aunt were as handsome as Buzz, especially in the picture of him wearing his dress blue navy uniform. The men who came to their table all seemed to have bad teeth, needed shaves and had yellow stains on their fingers. She didn't know how her aunt could stand them being near her, interrupting her as her fork was half way to her mouth. Some even asked her to dance while she chewed her food. She would dab at the corners of her mouth with a white cloth napkin. Radio Joe always handed it to her personally when she first sat down, as well as to Tess and the cronies. Then, as if she wrote the definitive work on etiquette, "I'm on vacation from dancing," she said her napkin going to her mouth to cover a slight cough. "Doctor's orders," was the polite reply coming from behind the napkin. Then the etiquette book would get shelved, and she would shovel a load of gravel from her throat. "I'm here to get a Musky, not a man." The Cutty Sark would disappear from her glass and she'd say, "I've had way too many men and not enough Musky." There would be laughter all around and then her aunt would daintily wipe the hand that had held the Scotch glass, place it lightly on Tess's, and give her a look that made her feel safe and secure. "Precious, you are having a good time, aren't you?"

"Oh, yes, Auntie," she responded, her enthusiasm making her bounce around on the hard wooden café chair. And she was having a good time, never knowing what to expect because her aunt was always surprising her. She couldn't wait for the next day and dinner to end because Aunt Rose promised her that they were going to a real Indian pow-wow and her new friend, Chief John Proud Bear had made the arrangements and promised Tess he would be there.

Chief John Proud Bear, who Radio Joe had hired as a guide to take Aunt Rose and her small party fishing, had Tess feeling she had known him her entire life. She hid behind her aunt, curious eyes peering out from behind her aunt's hip, the rest of her out of sight when she first saw him chatting with Mr. Radio. She saw Mr. Radio wave and heard him say: "Hey, Rose, I want you to meet the best Musky guide in all of Wisconsin." When her aunt started to walk toward the men Tess glued herself to her aunt's hip, shoveling along, trying to keep up with her.

"Rose," said Radio Joe smiling, "I'd like you to meet Chief John Proud Bear. If it's a Musky you want, John's your man."

Tess watched her aunt reach out and shake hands with a man who was different than anyone she had ever seen in her young life. "Nice to meet you, John," her aunt said. "It is John and not Chief or something like that."

Tess heard, "John is fine." The voice was strong and polite and seemed to bore into her soul. Then he said, "May I have the honor of addressing you as Rose?" Tess felt her aunt's body rock with laughter. "Honor any way you'd like," her aunt said. "If you get me a Musky, I'll honor you." Tess heard the three of them laugh. Then not knowing where she got the nerve, she stepped out from behind her aunt and stuck out her shaking hand. "Hello, Mr. Chief John Proud Bear, my name is Tess, but I only allow my Auntie Rose to call me Precious."

"Tess it will be," said Chief John Proud Bear, his hand swallowing her tiny one like Baby and Ruth ingesting a morsel of fish food.

Before Tess realized she was sitting in the back seat of the Cadillac sandwiched between her aunt and the Ojibwa chief.

She couldn't take her eyes off him as her mind fired off silent questions. "Are you really a bear? You don't look like one." Her eyes didn't blink; lashes stationary, at attention, her sign of respect mixed with awe. "Are you really a chief?" she asked firing off another question; "A real live Indian?"

Chief John Proud Bear, his eyes the shape and color of large walnuts, smiled at her and said, "I'm not really a bear, Tess."

Tess could only stare.

"I am, however, proud," he said. "I'm proud of my heritage, my people and who I am."

Tess didn't blink; couldn't blink.

"And I am a chief," he said, his pride coated with respect for his new young friend. He smiled at Tess and then looked out the car window saying, "Rose, fifteen more minutes and we'll be at Potato Lake. Then you can show me just how good a Musky fisherman you are."

* * * * *

Mr. Sid and Mr. Curly were in a round bottom row boat that looked like it was held together with a hundred coats of green paint. They trailed behind an identical green boat that held Tess, the guide and their boss; the difference being that their guide had a five horse power motor attached to the back of the boat. The motor had a polished metal gas tank on top that had seen better days and was possibly minus two of the five horses. Their boat had been towed out to the first spot for fishing about half way around the lake from where John Proud Bear had rented the two boats from a tiny resort. Mr. Curly was at the oars and it was obvious that he was better at vaudeville than rowing a boat. "Stop scaring the fish," Mr. Sid carped. "Those things in your hands are called oars and they're used to row;

not splash half the lake in our damned boat."

"Shut up and fish," retorted Mr. Curly as more water splashed into the boat.

Tess sat like a miniature statue in the bow of the boat, her aunt separating her from Chief John Proud Bear, her fishing rod clutched in a death grip across her lap. She jumped when she heard Chief John Proud Bear say to her, "Tess, there are no flying fish in Potato Lake." He smiled as he rested the oars in the water. "Hand me your rod and I'll put bait on it." Tess passed the rod to her aunt who then handed it to the Indian. In less than a minute, Tess had the cork handle of the fishing rod being choked by her hands and she returned to being a statue, her eyes the only part of her moving as she watched her line trail out behind her off the bow of the boat. She didn't know what to do and was afraid of being a pest to ask what to do with the rod and reel in her tiny hands. So, she sat and listened to her Aunt Rose who chatted continually with the Indian guide; her more with him than him with her. The boat was never silent; the idle chit-chat punctuated by the slight squeaking coming from the oar locks complaining; the hum from her aunt's casting reel never ceasing while periodic subdued laughter added to a day that was full of new experiences for Tess.

Aunt Rose seldom took a break from casting the large white buck tail with the brass colored spinner and fascinating treble hook, the bait landing exactly where she aimed it. When she did stop casting, a chrome platted thermos would appear from under her seat. She would fill the cup three quarters full, take a sip and then pass it to Chief John. He'd take a sip, nod his approval and pass it back as Tess's photo album continued to grow.

Tess, in her private nightly conversations with Patsy, referred to Chief John Bears as, "That Indian man is soooo nice," placing and emphasis on stretching out, so. "Aunt Rose always calls him Chief or Johnnie," she continued telling Patsy of the day's events.

And Tess was correct in her observations even noticing how often the thermos got passed back and forth. Not wanting to be a pest, she never asked her aunt and Chief John Bear what was in the thermos.

Tess, with Patsy squeezed in along side of her, sat motionless in the bow of a round bottom, wooden row boat that glided slowly along with each pull of the oars that barely made a ripple. Tess never asked why the boat moved backward and not forward. As time appeared to stand still, she got braver and shed her statue quality. She started playing pretend games that were dominated by a backdrop of the blue sky filled with puffy clouds, imagining she was adrift on the ocean waiting for Buzz and his Tin-Can to rescue her from a horde of monster Musky. Chief John continued to quietly dip the oars in the water. His pulling motion was almost invisible as the boat inched along the outside edge of the lily pads keeping a distance of about twenty five yards from the boat to the weed edge. His expressionless ongoing series of nods indicated to Aunt Rose where he wanted her to place her next cast. Tess would hold on to her fishing pole, the one her aunt had bought her, not watching the cork bobber that trailed away on the opposite side of where her aunt was casting. She was only slightly curious as to why a minnow was attached to a hook at the end of her line. She had Patsy, the photographs in her mind, views of bull rushes, the sky and hopes of Buzz joining her.

Tess had grown tired of fishing about the time Chief John Proud Bear had put the minnow on her hook and had her trail it from the bow of the boat. Being both bored and inquisitive, she lowered the tip of her pole into the water and began to slide it back and forth. That activity interested her for about thirty seconds. Then she submerged the pole into the water and watched the water cover the reel. Another thirty seconds went by and then she decided to hold the pole over her head and look up at the sky. She pretended the fishing pole was the antenna at Radio Joe's and she sat very still pretending to hear the voice of her father telling her, "Now don't you go being a little pest when you're with Rose."

It was later in the day, well into the afternoon, when she felt her fishing pole almost jerked from her tiny hands. She was having an in-depth conversation with Patsy; the doll resting in her lap, the fishing pole under the doll and both of her hands on the cork grip, but barely. That's when she felt the yank, the pole leaping from her lap and landing in the bottom of the boat along with a shocked and dazed Patsy. Tess had no idea how, at that moment, her life would change forever.

There was laughter from Aunt Rose and a stern look from Chief John who had wrapped his hand around her line that was trailing from the bow. He had yanked so hard that Tess almost jumped out of the boat.

"Lady of the blue sky," Chief John said in his soothing, deep voice, "the muskellunge possesses powerful magic and can cast a spell on those who don't pay attention." His dark, red lined eyes were kind, a smiling touch of twinkle doing a dance for her. He unwound the line from his hand, reset the minnow on the hook and tossed it back into the water. "Don't worry, Lady of the Blue Sky, he said, repeating the name that had also caught Aunt Rose's attention. "The muskellunge is no match for you and your papoose."

Tess gently picked up Patsy from the bottom of the boat and thought that Chief John was making fun of her by calling her, Lady of the Blue Sky. Then she noticed his eyes were even kinder and gentler than her father's and knew Chief John Proud Bear was sincere. She embraced her new name and shifted her attention between staying alert and keeping Patsy securely locked under her arm and squeezed into her side. Her attention lasted the usual thirty seconds and then strayed to the boat where Mr. Sid and Mr. Curly trailed behind them. They always seemed to be arguing, but Tess never understood about what. On the first day they couldn't agree on who would row with Mr. Curly saying, "What the hell does a New York Jew know about rowing a boat or fishing?"

She heard Mr. Sid respond, "I know lox; don't you?"

"Of course I know lox," Mr. Curly snapped back, "and herring too."

"Good," Mr. Sid said, shifting to the back seat of the boat and stretching his legs out forward, hands behind his head. "Now learn oars."

"Hey, Mr. Curly said sternly, "watch your mouth." Tess could see him nod in her direction. "Remember, there's a K-I-D present."

Mr. Sid pointed at the oars. "I said oars, you jerk. Not your sisters."

"Will you two stop," Aunt Rose yelled at them as she looked over her shoulder from the back of the row boat, her rod ready for the next cast. "Try to behave for a change," she continued, scolding them both as if they were a couple of bratty kids. "You'll scare the damn fish!"

Tess couldn't stop thinking about the name Chief John had given her and found herself totally enthralled with the Chief, not taking her eyes off him. She had been enamored with him from the very first meeting. At noon during that first day of fishing on Potato Lake, he had rowed their boat up to the shore on a sandy beach at lunch time. Curious, she trailed behind as he found a flat rock, stopped, and placed down a stringer of walleye he, Mr. Sid and Mr. Curly had caught. Aunt Rose had concentrated on getting her Musky. Tess hadn't caught a thing. She clutched Patsy and took several nervous steps back trying to stay out of the guide's sight. As if by magic, Chief John pulled out a large knife and Tess almost squeezed Patsy in half. She stood frozen in the sand, watching as he ran his thumb over the blade. Before she could comprehend what he was doing, the knife was stripping away the side of the first fish. She was fascinated with the speed of the knife and how easily the flesh vanished from each of the fish. The wide long blade glided through the stringer's contents until a pile of perfect fillets lay on the trunk of a fallen tree next to the flat rock. She continued to watch, the mental photographs mounting, extra pages being added to her album as the Indian put the fish remains in the lake. She was amazed at the sight of a skeleton, stomach cavity intact, complete with fins, tail and a head that seemed to swim in a school looking alive.

"Food for the eagles," said Chief Proud Bear without looking at her.

Tess looked at Patsy, her eyes asking the buttons: "How did he know we were here behind him?" Too afraid of being a pest and definitely in awe of the Indian, she stood like one of the straight trees and continued to watch as he squatted at the edge of the lake and rinsed the fillets. Before she knew it, he had gathered an arm load of branches from some of the really messy trees along the shore and built a fire. Then he turned and nodded that Tess should follow him. Obediently, she trailed after the Indian Chief to their boat where she watched him pull out a burlap potato sack from under the rear seat along with two cast iron skillets. He handed the skillets to Tess. Not anticipating the weight of the heavy skillets, she almost dropped them.

"Hey, Johnnie,'" she heard her Aunt Rose call out from where she was sitting on a log with Mr. Sid and Mr. Curly, "how 'bout a luncheon cocktail?" The noon sun glistened off the chrome thermos.

"When lunch is ready, Rose," he said, his deep calm voice commanding everyone's attention. "Right now, O-zah-wa-sko-gi-ji-go-kwe is going to learn how to prepare a shore lunch."

A tri-echoed question came from the log, "Who?"

"That's Ojibwa for Lady of the Blue Sky," Chief John said, his hand coming to rest on top of Tess's head for an instant like a gentle giant butterfly.

Chapter 7

The memory of her new name, one she stumbled through so many times before getting it right, would become the front cover of her photo album. A picture of her Aunt Rose, casting rod in hand, the ever present pearl cigarette holder and Pall Mall protruding from her mouth as she smiled would grace the inside front cover; Chief John Proud Bear teaching her how to fry fish for a shore lunch would be her first page.

The day would have been perfect had she caught a fish. She didn't even get a nibble. Tess jumped into bed that night without being told, pulled the covers up to her chin and said, "Good night, Aunt Rose."

Her aunt just smiled and shook her head from side to side several times. She bent down and gave Tess a goodnight kiss on the tip of her nose. Still smiling, her head continuing to go from side to side, Aunt Rose lit up a cigarette, turned out the bedroom light and said, "Goodnight, Blue Sky Lady."

Tess couldn't close her eyes. They were wider than Patsy's and she couldn't wait for the next day to see what awaited her. "I think Chief John's a very nice man, don't you," she said to Patsy. The sound of the river made her pull her doll closer to her. "I knew you'd like him too. And you know what, Patsy," she said looking into the button eyes that appeared to have grown wider as the trip progressed, "maybe Chief John will give you an Indian name just like mine." She gave her doll a squeeze. "Well, not like mine," she rattled on, talking so fast she couldn't get her new Indian name right no matter how many times she repeated it. "Yours will be different."

Tess bolted out of bed the next morning when her aunt gently nudged her. She was half way to the tiny bathroom with the rust stains on the sink and toilet bowl when she stopped, came back and got Patsy.

"You really are a precious one you are," her aunt said.

Then there was the familiar, intriguing sound of a scratching match, the smell of sulfur and her aunt inhaling, but Tess didn't care. She sensed a special magic as she walked to the lodge for breakfast with her aunt, a faint smell of smoke from the lodge's fieldstone fireplace enticing them along. In the dining room, she couldn't wait for breakfast to end so that she could be in the boat with Chief John. "Aunt Rose, are we going to leave for Potato Lake soon?" she asked trying to be polite.

"Precious," said her aunt putting down her coffee cup then inserting another cigarette into the holder as if performing delicate surgery. "Today we're going to Ghost Lake."

"Ghost, Auntie?" she asked, feeling for Patsy alongside of her chair.

"Yep, Precious," her aunt said, reaching out and patting Tess on her cheek. "Chief John says there's a big Musky there with my name on it."

"Are real ghosts there, Auntie?"

Her aunt smiled and patted her hand. "It's just the name of a lake, Precious. Don't worry about any ghosts."

Tess wanted to believe her aunt, wanted Patsy to believe her aunt, but she had her doubts. She began to feel better when she realized her new friend Chief John would be there to protect her.

* * * * *

Chief John rented two boats from an elderly lady who resembled Tess's grandmother. The lady owned a tiny general store on Ghost Lake, and her grey hair was in the process of receiving a home permanent when the dust streaked and insect splattered Cadillac pulled up. She wore a faded, light blue house dress with tiny nondescript flowers on it, the upper half covered with what was once a plastic table cloth to protect her from the foul smelling hair solution. Tess stood by the car and watched her Aunt Rose walk guardedly toward the window of the general store. There was a small flag with a single star in the middle hanging solemnly. She looked at the elderly woman then turned her head slightly so the flag was in her view. "Her mother," she said, nodding ever so slightly in Tess's direction, "has two of those in her front room window." Nothing more was said.

Chief John, who appeared propped up between two sets of boat oars next to the Cadillac, glanced toward Mr. Sid and Mr. Curly and then toward the lake. "Musky aren't like frogs," he said, his usual calm baritone voice getting their attention. He picked up both sets of oars put them under one arm and grabbed Aunt Rose's fishing tackle box. "No legs. You have to come to them." He started for the lake.

Tess's dream for an exciting day with Chief John began before her aunt could even make her first cast. The Indian had just put a minnow on the end of Tess's line and flipped it into the water when her cork bobber vanished and her line zipped through the water away from the boat. Patsy found herself on the bottom of the boat as Tess's tiny hands cranked at the reel and her front teeth dug into her lower lip.

"Don't give him any slack," she heard her aunt say, but didn't know what she meant.

Then Chief John said, "Slowly swing your rod toward me."

She did, amazed at the strength hidden under the water. There was a swirl, a splash of water, and Chief John reached down grabbing the fish with his bare hand. "Is that a mean old Musky?" she asked excited and out of breath.

"Walleye," Chief John said, the fish sliding down a yellow stained, thin rope stringer. "Also lunch for you, said the Chief."

She didn't know what to say when she heard her Aunt Rose exclaim, "Jesus, John, you've got the fastest hands I've ever seen." She continued to admire Tess's catch as the Indian placed the fish in the water and tied the rope stringer around the seat brace next to him. "And, believe me, in my time I've seen some mighty fast ones."

In the next hour, Tess caught eight more Walleye, prompting Chief John to say, "The spirit of the blue sky is proud of you for providing lunch for all of us."

"I can catch more, "Tess said bubbling over, "I know I can."

"The spirit thinks not," Chief John said, glancing up at the sky and nodding toward the southwest.

"But I can," Tess insisted, brimming with confidence. "I really can." Then she heard the thunder.

"The spirit speaks the truth," Chief John said, pulling in her line and extending his open hand toward her. Reluctantly she handed him her pole. "Miss Rose," he said, looking toward shore as another clap of thunder rolled across the lake and the sky began to darken pushing away the sunshine as an ugly black took its place. Rose had her line in and rod positioned on the seat next to her before the next explosion of thunder. This one was even louder, a deep rumbling roar, and Chief John raised his right hand, his index finger pointing toward the shore. Tess could see Mr. Sid and Mr. Curly pull in their lines and Mr. Sid wrestling with the oars. With several powerful strokes of the oars, Chief John had spun the boat around, pointed the bow toward the shore, pushed on the oars with a grunt and had it cutting a bubbling path through the lily pads toward the stretch of sand beach of a small bay. Tess jumped as a bolt of lightning vanished into the trees lining the bay where they were headed. The noise hurt her ears and she pulled Patsy close to her when she noticed Chief John nod at her aunt. In a moment Aunt Rose had a duffle bag from under her seat, opened it, and handed a small bundle tied with a leather lace to Chief John. "Here," he said, handing the bundle to Tess, the leather lace lying across his lap, "put this on."

She had never worn a rain poncho before, and it was much too big for her and Patsy. Her face was barely visible through the opening in the hood. She watched as her aunt put her own poncho on just as the boat scraped against the sand and gravel bottom. Chief John stood up just as the first drop of rain bounced off the hood of Tess's poncho. She watched as the Indian stepped out of the boat, water almost to the top of his worn, scuffed leather fishing boots and pulled the boat half way on the shore. In the next instant he had lifted Tess from the boat, placing her on the shore, and then took Aunt Rose's hand as the boat rolled slightly from side to side with each step she took. Mr. Sid and Mr. Curly's boat came scraping to shore just as the heaven's opened and, as Tess's father had once described to her, "The angels are bowling."

Chief John went about his business oblivious to the rain. He pulled up the collar of his red plaid, wool shirt and slid a piece of folded canvas from under the back seat of the second boat beached next to theirs. In a few short minutes he had built a rain shelter, and the four fishermen huddle under the canvas roof. Tess watched as Chief John went to their boat and took out the same burlap bag and the two cast iron skillets. In a moment she was scurrying down the beach with her hands out, almost tripping on the poncho. She saw the smile on Chief John's face as he handed her the skillets and they both made their way back to the shelter. He patted Tess on the head and made sure she was in the middle of the tent shelter that sounded as if they rain would punch holes in it. There was his smile and he headed into the woods.

"Well," Aunt Rose said sounding disappointed, "it looks like that big Musky turned into a cat with nine lives." She unscrewed the cap from the thermos, took a long sip and then passed it to Mr. Curly. Just as he passed the thermos to Mr. Sid, Chief John emerged from the woods dragging what appeared to be half of the Northwoods with him.

"Hey, Chief," Mr. Sid yelled out holding the thermos aloft, "a slug of fire water before lunch?"

The Indian shrugged and went about building what appeared to be a circle made of logs and covered with an umbrella of branches. He filled the circle with kindling and carefully arranged larger pieces of branches which he systematically snapped into the desired lengths by stepping on them with his boots.

"Johnnie," Rose called out from under the protection of the canvas shelter, "you're not planning to rub two sticks together in this rain, are you?"

Chief John smiled as he walked past the canvas shelter, his head going from side to side as he quickly headed toward their boat, the rain poking tiny craters into the sand. He walked into the water, again to the top of his boots, and grabbed a red gallon can from the stern of the boat without breaking stride. As he walked back to the circle of wood he unscrewed the cap from the can placing the scratched dented cap in his shirt pocket. The contents of the can splashed on the small pile of wood and Chief John stepped back, screwed the lid back on the spout and placed the can on the ground away from the circle. His fingers pulled a small cylindrical container from the breast pocket of his wool shirt. He unscrewed the cap and, before they all realized what he was doing there was a loud *whoosh*. Flames leapt out and up licking at the protective roof of leaves over the circle. Chief John turned and looked at the group huddled in the shelter. "I only need to rub one stick, Rose," he said, his twinkling eyes visible through the down pour. "Indian rain stick."

Tess had left the cover of the rain shelter and was at Chief John's side ready to help. As she had seen him do before, Chief John filleted the fish and submerged each in one of the skillets filled with hot, steaming bacon grease that popped and cracked from the droplets of rain working their way through the crude roof over the fire. Cubed potatoes with chunks of onion steamed and sizzled in the other skillet while two tin cans of beans, their lids pried open from Chief John's buck knife, bubbled softly alongside the edge of the fire. Several mosquitoes and a deer fly found the grease and Chief John flicked them out with the tip of his large knife.

Over the years, Tess remembered that as being one of the

best meals she ever had. Way too many times she had told her daughters about the insects cooking in the skillets which she had carried for Chief John. Her daughters, one newly arrived to adolescence and the other on the brink, always rolled their eyes. They did, however, show signs that they were listening when their mother told them for the first time about the Indian pow-wow and how Chief John Proud Bear had called her in front of the tribal members of the Lac Court Oreilles band of Ojibwa and made her an honorary member giving her the permanent name of O-zah-wa-sko-gi-ji-go-kwe.

"And then," she said to her daughters, eyes not moving, showing a folded piece of deer skin held lovingly in her hands, "Chief John Proud Bear presented me this." Her fingers meticulously unfolded the irregular shaped tan square unveiling a beaded head band with an eagle feather attached. Eyes were riveted to the feather. "This," she said proudly, holding up the head band and placing the deer skin aside, "makes me a sister to all Ojibwa." She carefully put on the head band waiting for the giggles that did not come and began to describe the Indian pow-wow.

"There was a circle of big logs, bigger than our house, where spectators sat watching tribal members do their traditional dances, moccasins barely beating the ground, feathered head dresses floating to the beat of tom-toms."

"Like the movies?" her youngest asked.

"Better."

"What happened then, Mom?" asked the oldest, her eyes unable to roll.

"Two Indian women came to where I was sitting with my Aunt Rose and escorted me by both hands into the center of the circle where I was invited to dance the celebration of adoption."

"You danced with real Indians?" both of her daughters asked at once.

Tess nodded her head. "The tom-toms took on a different beat, and the drummers began chanting," she said, her narrative good enough to be broadcast. "I thought my heart would jump out of my skin. I looked at the two women, and they gave me a subtle gesture that I should do what they were doing. My feet moved to the beat of those drums as if they had been doing it all of my life." Her soul smiled and she knew she was no longer, Oh, Mother; no longer the recipient of adolescent eye rolls. She was O-zah-wa-sko-gi-ji-go-kwe and her heart soared like the Eagle's feather on her head band once did.

That night, long ago, after the dancing had ended, Little Tess never saw her Aunt Rose hand Chief John a brown paper bag, inside a ten-dollar bill and a bottle of Old Granddad.

Chapter 8

Now Tess had another vivid memory of her vacation; this one starting a second and much shorter, photo album. It began just after she had returned home from the thirteen hour ride from Hayward and saw her mother. At first she thought she was looking at her grandmother. Then she was told that her father had been wounded and was coming home and that Buzz's Tin-Can had been hit during what she heard called a Kamikaze attack off Okinawa. "He's missing," she heard her mother's choked words to Aunt Rose.

"He'll turn up safe and sound," she heard her aunt say to her mother as the two hugged and held each other. "You know where to reach me if you need anything."

Her mother dabbed at her eyes with a stained handkerchief and mumbled, "I know."

"And don't be afraid to call on Tess," Aunt Rose said, putting her arm around Tess's shoulder and pulled her close, a long tender hug followed. "She's quite a grown up lady now."

* * * * *

It had been those memories of her Aunt Rose, Mr. Sid, Mr. Curly, Mr. Radio, and Chief John Proud Bear in that very special place so far away that had helped her through her own rough times many years later. The crooked, the messy and the straight showed their tough side and why a Musky would wrap her Aunt Rose's line around them. Peace didn't come easy for

Tess; nor did life. There were no allied forces and atomic bombs to help fight her battles. All she had was the giant photo album packed with memories of her vacation; her adoration for her Aunt Rose and for Chief John Proud Bear. They were the only human beings she ever elevated to the status of *Idol*. Actors, actresses, singers and celebrities may have been in the glow of their spotlights, but Tess's two idols generated their own almost blinding illumination.

Tess learned not too much later after her vacation with her aunt that her scrapbook needed three additional pages; her father and brothers each got their own page. Her father was never the same when he returned home from the war. Missing was his warm smile and his hugs. He just seemed to stare and hardly ever said a word. Buzz was finally reported killed in action just two days after Aunt Rose and her cronies had started their drive back to New York. Donny's page made an appearance a couple of years later. He had decided to attend Quigley Prep Seminary and become a priest.

As a budding pre-adolescent, Tess worked two part-time jobs and helped her mother, her father unable to do much after having pieces of shrapnel removed from the side of his head along with an ear. She tried to glue only the pictures of her father from before the war into her book, but her father's silent stare still appeared on the pages. Tess had emerged from adolescence and gotten married only to find her middle class American dream get flicked away like the insects in the hot, spitting bacon grease filled skillets of a shore lunch. The flicking, so to speak, came after her husband left her for another woman, but not before using her like the dark brown leather chug-a-luck dice cup her Aunt Rose would slam down on the bar taking turns with Radio Joe and her cronies playing for drinks. Her husband's slams came at least twice a week; whether she needed it or not. Then, realizing she didn't need a life filled with thunder and lightning a million times worse that the storm of long ago that forced her into a poncho, divorce and an order of protection followed. She raised two girls by herself, turning down offers for dates, finding herself alone, mostly in front of the television while hugging a pillow she called Patsy. There were many nights when she had conversations with the memory of her Aunt Rose, smelling her cigarettes and listening to her gravel voiced pep talks. They were together again, only she was an adult, but still Precious to her aunt. Tess would talk to her aunt, always at night when the girls were in bed. She would sit in the wingback chair in the living room of the small house in Elmwood Park near St. Celestine's Church. She had managed to hang on to her home after a vicious divorce that saw her husband being escorted away in hand cuffs after ignoring one too many court orders to stay away from her. She would tell Aunt Rose about how her girls had become latch-key kids. Aunt Rose disapproved. She told her aunt about the small Victory Garden she had kept in their backyard, canning vegetable like her mother. "Honest," she said to her aunt. "I had to tell my skeptical daughters, while crossing my heart with my right index finger, that it really was called a Victory Garden." There had been no world war, just her own battle to survive and, as she told the image of Aunt Rose, "I was trying to keep the bill collectors away from the door like Mr. Sid, Mr. Curly and Mr. Radio tried to keep those lecherous drunks away from you."

Her aunt understood, always understanding without saying

a word.

She thought she heard her aunt say, "You should've sent them to bed hungry a couple of nights. That would have ended their skepticism." There was the gravel sounding cough and her aunt saying, "Too bad they couldn't have viewed the carnage I saw when I went on tour to entertain our troops in Europe. If they had witnessed for one minute, seeing, hearing and smelling the results of unbelievable mayhem the way I did, you would have had two less rebels without a cause."

Tess agreed with her aunt, saying, "Hind sight is always twenty-twenty." She laughed, hers with a faint touch of gravel, sounding almost like her Aunt Rose. "I finally learned how to shrug off their comments by warning them that one day, the spirit of the blue sky would make believers of them."

Aunt Rose smiled when she heard that. She didn't smile when she first heard what Tess's daughters had said to their mother about going to Hayward, Wisconsin on a vacation and how they said it.

"Sure, Mom," the eleven year old had said.

"Right, Mom," the older one said, then adding. "Or Princess owah-wah or whatever that Indian name was you told us about."

"Don't you dare mock me," Tess had said, her words making the mental image of Aunt Rose take notice and even making adolescent deaf ears get the message. "Like it or not, you girls are going on a little vacation with your mother."

She had planned the trip for almost a year, excited most of the time, but sad because she knew Aunt Rose wouldn't be with them and there would be no Mr. Sid to buy her girls Cokes and Mr. Curly to sneak them Hershey bars or Baby Ruth's; and no Radio Joe to give them their first taste of caviar. Then she smiled knowing that Aunt Rose would be with them in spirit. Her plans were almost abandoned when she had contacted the Hayward Tourist Bureau and found out that there was no Radio Joe's. Contact with the local library and a librarian enthralled with her story, had Tess learning that Radio Joe had passed away and that his scary cabin, and all the other cabins and the radio tower were no more. It had disappeared after a brief tenure of ownership with Radio Joe's son, Eddie who was nicknamed, Television Eddie after the new invention that had pushed radio from the limelight. Only the main lodge was there and it was called the Wild River Inn; still situated near the eastern bank of the Namakagon River.

Tess could still see the kind, knowing eyes of Chief John Proud Bear looking into hers and felt her confidence returning. There was his nod of approval and the smile of his dark eyes saying, "Lady of the blue sky, the spirits make your vacation so."

Two final elements still needed to be solved for the vacation to Wisconsin. She shook off the disappointment of no Radio Joe's Resort for her girls to experience. There would be other resorts. Her biggest challenge was telling the girls that she really was serious about the vacation and that they were going.

"You're going and that's it," she had said to them, sounding like a combination of her mother and Aunt Rose on their most authoritarian days and feeling good about it. "You can pick where we're going to stay."

Her daughters sat in gloomy silence after their complaints had been shredded by a series of their mother's, "Because I said so." They listened to the names of unappealing places, each preceded by their mother's words, "What do you think of...?"

"Spider Lake?"

"Yuck."

"Clam Lake?"

"Oh, Yuck."

"Moose Lake?"

"Yucky."

"Teal Lake, Lost Lake, The Tiger Cat Flowage, Potato Lake?"

"You want us to stay on a lake named after a potato?" the oldest asked then adding in a disgusted tone, "That's the yuckiest of the yucky."

"I did," she said, her tone of voice much different than when she had asked her aunt about a lake named after a vegetable. "My Aunt Rose took me fishing there."

"Oh, please," the youngest said her nose almost swallowed up by wrinkles. "How could you even mention being associated with that so-called famous aunt of yours who paraded around in front of men in her underwear?" There was a pause followed by, "That's not yucky; that's gross."

Tess ignored her daughter's sarcasm letting it roll off her like the rain off the canvas shelter that Chief John Bear had built so many photo album pages ago. "What do you think of Ghost Lake?"

"All of my friends will laugh at me," the oldest said, her nose all but vanishing.

They reluctantly agreed on staying at a motel, and they could go wherever they wanted each day. Tess secretly felt that she had won since the motel she picked was near the site of Radio Joe's old resort.

As she drove her martyred daughters north that summer, she prayed that Chief John Proud Bear would still be alive. She had called information before they left and discovered that there was a number listed for his name. A nervous phone call produced a series of unanswered rings, but she still remained optimistic, just like her Aunt Rose's quest for a Musky. Her aunt finally did catch her Musky the last day of that war-time vacation.

* * * * *

"If Johnnie can't get me a Musky on the Chippewa Flowage, nobody can!" She remembered her aunt saying emphatically that night as she slid under the covers. The empty chrome thermos stood guard on the night stand in the cabin's bedroom as her aunt switched off the small lamp.

"Is that another lake, Aunt Rose?"

Her question was answered by her aunt's snoring.

It was the biggest fish Tess had ever seen, saying to Patsy as she watched her aunt and Chief John, "I'm not getting near that mean old monster." She recalled how her aunt looked knowingly at Chief John who held up his thumb and index finger, a ray of light barely showing through.

Chief John Bear shook his head and said, "Not quite an inch short, Rose."

"Pretty color though," Aunt Rose said, as she admired the fish. "Beautiful stripes and a great fighter," she continued the admiration showing in her voice. "Did you see him clear the water on that jump?"

"That's a Tiger Musky for you," Chief John said, holding up the catch for a moment longer. He carefully slipped the glistening fish back into the waters of the Chippewa Flowage on that last day. "He'll grow bigger and stronger and be waiting for you next year, Rose."

Chapter 9

There was no next year after that. Wars came and went. The adults she had known were all gone, younger generations taking up the march, joining the parade. That next year took way too long to get there, but it was finally here for her as she listened to her eleven year old say tentatively from the back seat where she had been sitting quietly ready her sister's teen magazines, "Mom, do you think I can have an Indian name?" Before Tess could answer, her older daughter replied, "Yeah. The Indians will call you Little Pain in the Butt."

"Oh, yeah," came the reply from the opposite side of the back seat. "And the Indians will call you, Squaw With No Boobs."

Tess tried to hide her smile, warning, "Enough you two." She knew that the special place she had known, the one that filled the photo album of her mind, would not be the same. That could never be recreated, but, she hoped and prayed her daughters would experience their own prized photographs and maybe, in her wildest dreams, find their own idols to guide them. Her hopes were fortified by a simple, silent prayer she repeated over and over during the hours of the trip now shortened by the Interstate system. "Please, dear God, let them meet Chief John Proud Bear."

* * * * *

Her days of being called, Precious were long gone, turned to dust and never to be experienced again. Nothing, not even the brutality of a sad, sick husband could wipe out the memories of her being referred to as, Precious by her Aunt Rose. All of the actors were gone from that special week in her life; all but one she prayed.

Tess knew that replicating those times could never be, not even God or fate could do that, but she was determined enough to provide enough props for her daughters' imaginations to catch hold. Fishing poles were packed in the car's trunk. She had picked them up at her mother's house on a whim years earlier sensing they would be needed some day. The fishing rods had been stored in the dark, dank basement and even her brother Donny, who had left the priesthood and lived with his mother, didn't know they were there. Then her mother had gone into a nursing home and she and her brother sold the Logan Square house. A third fishing rod in the trunk had been a gift that Aunt Rose had given her. Also stashed in the trunk of the car, wrapped in an old burlap bag, were two cast iron skillets she had purchased at a garage sale for a dollar each. "It's going to work out," she said to herself as they entered Sawyer County. "I just know it is. It has to."

She was worn out from the drive and wondering how Mr. Sid and Mr. Curly had managed the trip without an Interstate highway to speed them along. Adrenalin pushed aside exhaustion and a chronic sore back, an unwanted memory of her ex, now late, husband. The girls surprised her, unpacking the car without her having to order them to do so when they got to the motel. She notice a change in her girls the moment they stepped out of the car and found themselves in the middle of more pine trees they ever knew existed; pleased at the curious looks on their faces as they eyed the surroundings; seeing that they were not on the narrow, tree lined streets of Elmwood Park looking at octagon brick bungalows.

Sitting on the edge of the bed with a too hard mattress, Tess paged through the local phone book comprising a dozen or so communities. Her heart jumped when she saw the name of John Proud Bear. She took a slip of paper from her purse and compared the phone numbers. "It's him," she muttered as her daughters watched in silence. She took a deep breath, exhaled slowly and her noticeably trembling index finger began punching in digits. The phone rang and rang, and she began to feel her hopes fading. Then she heard the voice. "Is this Chief John Proud Bear?" she asked, her stomach churning faster than on the day long ago when she reeled in her first fish. She sat motionless, silent.

Her oldest daughter finally prompted her, "God, Mom, say something before he hangs up."

"Chief John Proud Bear," she said cautiously, pausing again, her words lodged in her throat.

"Mother, the youngest one said in a frustrated whisper, "say something."

Chief John Proud Bear, this is Te..." She stopped and swallowed. An agonizing silence began to blanket the room until she said, "This is O-zah-wa-sko-gi-ji-go-kwe." She listened and began to smile, moist eyes overfilling. Gone were the crooked and messy trees of her life. Gone was the thunder and lightning that accompanied the rain that fell way too often and the wind that blew way too hard trying to break her rigid bull rush spine. With Aunt Rose's help, she only bent. "I idolized you, Auntie Rose," she said to herself. "You were my strength.

You were my idol; my hero; you and Chief John."

Her hand slid a few inches across the bed spread and came to rest next to the burlap bag that her youngest had placed on the bed earlier. "Two," she said, as her fingers traced the skillet handles through the rough fabric. "I'd like for you to meet them." A laugh worked its way through her tears as she said, "Of course I'm a better fisherman than they are. I had the two greatest teachers in the world."

She listened not glancing at her daughters who had snuggled up to her, one on the right and the other on the left. Her head barely nodded. "We'll be there, Chief John."

Once again she was Precious holding her Patsy. There were the aromas of Radio Joe's and the sounds of the Namakagon River. Sturdy bull rushes smiled at her. The messy and the crooked trees reached out and hugged the Lady of the Blue Sky welcoming her home.

Author's Note:

The name, Lady of the Blue Sky was culled from an article that appeared in The Lakeland Times, Minocqua, Wisconsin years ago and was taken from the file cabinet of the author's mind for this novella.

PART II

The One That Got Away

Chapter 1

Stan had two heroes in his life; his mother's father, Grandpa Zev and his dad's father, Gramps. He idolized the oft cantankerous grandfathers who were like magical glue that held his life together after a maple tree, a fish and a worn address book tried to shatter it.

Stan had kept his unique version of a little black book way too long. The single, dog eared page with tinges of yellow eroding the edges had one entry printed in Olde English script, *El B*. The blazing torch he carried for her over the years had burned down to a rare spark coughing its way to extinction, barely casting a flickering glow on his once love like the last bulb on a dying neon sign. Stan thought he had let her go. A small recess of his heart begged to differ. He had lived in his dim dream world for what seemed like forever, beating himself up; convinced he was at fault. He had chased her away; his rigid life's agenda staying on track shouting out his message: *Year One, Going Steady; Year Two, Engaged; Year Three, Love and Marriage.*

El B may have heard Stan's message, but she didn't listen or, didn't like what she heard. Then she gave him a message.

Stan couldn't believe what he heard. He listened and didn't want to believe. How could she not like him? That fact, though untrue, was one of many conjured up in his overactive mind. Another scenario escaping from his grey matter involved his grand plot to get her back. That scheme was complete with prayers and ended with Stan discovering that all the King's horses and all the King's men couldn't put his shattered heart together again.

Over time, Stan's torch coughed and sputtered until the sparks took a last gasp along with his plotting, praying and pretending. There was a final wisp of smoke and he stopped looking. At least he convinced himself he had.

Stan's life after *El B*, or Johanna Diana Pearson as her immigrant parents from Sweden had christened her, became ruled by another pocket address book; this a red one with gold gilded edging; the pages jammed with a collection of female names placed in his unique alphabetized system. His major criteria for a feminine name to be inscribed on a sacred page of his Holy Grail of Physiological Gratification was that the lady had to have a face that would qualify her to appear on the cover of a fashion magazine. Other attributes, in his order of importance, were a body that would grace the pages of the "Sports Illustrated" Swimsuit Edition, cause jaws to drop and eyes to pop out. A personality that included a funny bone, one that thrived on British humor as his did, was paramount. Secretly, all he wanted was an old fashioned girl with a family background that gave hints of her being worthy to be the mother of his children. He sorted the women in his address book by hair color. The opening pages started with names of ladies with auburn colored hair. A collection of black haired beauties appeared next. Then came the blonds; an array starting with ash and ending with strawberry; bottle jobs were inserted in a separate category. There were no dumb ones. *El B* had been a blond, a bottle job one, but her name was not listed. Brunettes followed the blonds. Redheads, real not dyed, took up a full page. His alphabetical categories ended with coiffures and color combinations that didn't fit into his rigid system. Each name in his book had at least one phone number, sometimes two or three and, the ones he deemed special, their address. He had even recorded several birthdays. Along side of each name was a series of two to five black dots; his version of a five star rating system. A single dark line drawn through a name took the place of one black dot. He had only drawn a single line through a name once. A stunning fashion model wearing more than white face powder under her nose found herself eradicated. She never knew. Dope was on his taboo list. According to Stan's rigid belief system, dope was for dopes and any substance user, alcohol excluded, should be exiled to Molokai to suffer under the sympathetic eyes of Father Damien. No girl he ever went out with got less than two dots. None of them, alone or collectively, ever got his highest rating of a fifth dot. That was given out only once in his life, back before the red book, when Johanna loved him. Then there weren't enough dots in the world. Had his rating system been based solely on sex, several entrants would have had soared past his five scale, receiving perfect tens and *El B* would not have been one of them. He had no way, however, of making a comparison. His relationship with Johanna hadn't progressed to the stage of, *going all the way* as it was known by his generation. They had come close, but had managed to come up for air in time, gasping and frustrated. As passionate as he was for her, his belief system kept him in check. Stan believed that when his bride-to-be walked down the aisle wearing white, that dress was more than a fashion statement covering hypocrisy. Then a maple tree with a heart carved in its trunk was cast aside and replaced by a red address book and collection of dots. All beliefs in virtue and virginity got swept away. The number of pages in his red book added up while his black book still contained the lonely page enshrining Einar and Annamargret Pearson's daughter.

Chapter 2

He never could rid himself of what happened that last day with Johanna. He tried. The nightmare of that afternoon never totally left him; the final sight of her, albeit her back and a pony tail swishing a farewell statement: "Get lost!" refused to be purged. The sound of a front door being slammed shut and her exit from his life stayed way too vivid for way too long. It was like the words from songs that weren't so gentle on his mind, those back roads of his memories filled with muddy ruts and detour signs. He was eighteen then, a college man, the eager freshman chomping at the bit and ready for a career, in the business world he thought, but didn't know why. What he did know was that he was in love and that meant he was primed to enter the world of adults joining the ranks of future husbands and providers, even fathers.

Johanna had been a year younger than Stan, having just sashayed from sweet sixteen and one month into her senior year in high school. As the song went, "She was seventeen, a hotrod queen and the prettiest gal he had ever seen." Stan had no clue that his being primed for entry into where older people resided did not coincide with Johanna's. Why would it? She was his steady girl and a steady girl, well, went along with what a steady boyfriend did and wanted. That's what all the love songs said; the ones he listened to; the ones that didn't belabor the point about breaking up being very hard to do. He wasn't concerned with moments to remember. Why would he be? He was living in the present, his Garden of Eden perfect and he savored every moment. So did, he thought, Johanna. She savored, but not with him, creating her own moments to remember that didn't include Stan.

* * * * *

What was to be their last date, unbeknownst to Stan, had undergone several alterations; none of which would ever be pasted into a scrapbook for safe keeping. Stan had planned an old fashioned picnic in the forest preserve complete with his Aunt Gert's old wicker basket filled with food and her red and black plaid wool blanket that saw many a Notre Dame Football game in South Bend. It was the fall season and the colors were at their bonfire best. The picnic basket would also contain a thermos filled with icy lemonade that he had spiked with gin from a dusty bottle he had found at home under the basement steps behind a stack of paint cans. The gin bottle, he remembered, had belonged to his late grandfather, his mother's father who, as the oft told embellished story went, walked from his native Belgium to America escaping from the German army. He was a young boy barely in his teens and Stan soaked up every word of the treacherous journey. Stan remembered his Grandpa Zev, a shortened version of his Belgium name, with the admiration reserved for idols like movie stars and sports heroes.

Grandpa Zev had been a cantankerous old geezer. That's how Stan's father described him. Grandpa, a widower and once proud house painter now with arthritic hands resembling knotted fists, had come to live with his daughter's family out of necessity. He joked continuously about not remembering to zip up. Then the joking stopped when he began to forget to zip down.

Grandpa Zev, Stan remembered vividly, made his own gin in a five gallon crock. The crock was also used for making dill pickles and several batches of sauerkraut. His grandfather would inform everyone in the family with a daily toast, his juice glass embossed with picture of a plump orange with two green accent leaves and filled to the brim. His glass held high in a hand showing signs of tremors greeted whoever entered the kitchen where he sat at one end of a mahogany drop leaf table butted up against a bare wall. Grandpa Zev would say in a voice that sounded like a cheap tenor with laryngitis, "A juniper berry a day keeps the doctor away." Many in his family agreed saying that Grandpa never got sick because he was always pickled. Grandpa, who wasn't supposed to drink because of a number of other ailments that should have had him in his grave years earlier, hid his homemade booze in a number of clear, screw capped bottles stashing them throughout the house. His favorite places were the damp basement during the winter months and the garage during the summer. He gave up on the garage during the winter because the snow showed the path he cut back and forth to the house and, one night, he almost froze to death. That was after he had too many nips from whatever container he imbibed from and fell asleep in his son-in-law's Nash sedan. He was found later that night slumped over the steering wheel suffering from hypothermia. His son-in-law originally thought Grandpa took his life by ingesting a garage full of oily exhaust fumes from the Nash. Then he remembered the car's battery was being charged on his workbench and that Grandpa Zev had charged his own battery.

Chapter 3

Stan's picnic suggestion to Johanna was actually a carefully orchestrated subterfuge; an intricate plan to cover up a surprise he had prepared for her; the spiked lemonade possibly creating a twist or two for when she thanked him for being so creative with his surprise. He never anticipated that *El B* had her own creative ways to respond to his creativity; hers filled with disgust along with a volley of degradation being spit back in his face; her depositing his high school class ring in the palm of his hand.

"Picnic?" she had repeated, making the word sound like it consisted of an army of ants crawling up her legs which she thought were too chunky, but perfect to Stan. "Who goes on picnics?" she asked the expression on her face stating it wouldn't take much more of his presence to make her throw up. "Old people go on picnics," she continued showing no signs of stopping. "Gawd, Stan, all you see at picnics are fat people eating and drinking too much and unruly children running around screaming and wearing most of their food on their clothing."

When she finished destroying his surprise with other assorted barbs running the gamut from juvenile too stupid to, and a first for her, asinine, he felt he needed a dictionary to counter her negative parts. He thought he heard, disdain along with mockery and boredom; each verbal slap coated with what he couldn't believe were assorted veneers of anger and hatred.

His surprise for her had quickly fallen into a category of no date at all. He found himself begging and pleading, suggesting, "How 'bout we go for a ride and stop at that ice cream store you like. I'll buy you a peppermint ice cream cone. You know how you like peppermint ice cream." He had never groveled before. "And, then, maybe we could go for a walk like we used to. You used to love to go for walks. Maybe in the forest preserve somewhere." He had worked too long and too hard on his surprise for her and planned to carefully on concealing his spiked lemonade under a bushel basket in the garage. He wasn't about to be denied. "We can look at the fall colors," he said trying to sound chipper, but unable to come out with half a chip. She reluctantly agreed and Stan's life recovered from the final death of a fall season to blossoming into springtime again. He opened his car door for her and she reluctantly got in, arms automatically crossing her chest and staying that way. He didn't notice that she sat almost wedged between her seat and the passenger side door. Maybe he would have if his mind hadn't been locked on his surprise and the thermos of spiked lemonade now stashed under the driver's side front seat.

* * * * *

Their walk to look at the changing leaves had started at the tail end of a hating-to-let-go Indian summer. The ride seemed to loosen her up. At least her arms appeared to swing easily as she walked, her setting a pace that made it seem she was on a mission. He strained to keep slightly ahead of her trying to lead the way; feeling he was about to start jogging. She talked and he listened. He continued to listen but realized he heard nothing. She never brought up their relationship; how long they had gone steady and what their future together would be once she was through with high school that year. He didn't care what she said, listening to her always made him feel good. They kept walking across the picnic grove, their pace throttling down. He took a glance back to where he had parked in the narrow paved lot, leaves hiding the lines. It didn't matter. His was the only car. They continued walking in a diagonal direction toward the far end of the vast picnic area where the trees created a natural border. Her talking suddenly stopped and she became very quiet, the only sound coming from her feet crushing the dying leaves. Their walk had turned into a crawl and they seemed oblivious to Mother Nature's kaleidoscope blazing from the wall of trees. He took her by the hand and inched forward before stopping in front of a majestic sugar maple. His hand released hers and went around her waist, his other hand, index finger extended out, began to trace his creation in the trunk of the tree, following the outline of a heart. "Surprise!" he blurted out, a gigantic smile almost swallowing the love coming from his eyes.

She looked at him as if he had stepped off a space ship.

"Do you like it?" he asked, his question filled with love and oblivious to his alien status.

"Like what?" she questioned, her reply filled with nothing.

His index finger did an emphatic point landing on the intricately carved initials in the middle of a perfectly symmetrical artistically etched heart. "The *El B's*," he said, sounding pleased, his finger tracing the initials and then, jokingly, referring to the nicknames that Johanna's older sister had given to them, "*El Beasto* and *El Breasto*, the Beast and the Breast," he said. Then continuing lovingly he said, "The *B's* for all eternity." The arm around her waist pulled her to him and he expected one of her playful hugs.

She didn't budge. Instead, she sarcastically said, "For all eternity?" The expression on her face was as alien to him as his new status was to her and said everything that needed to said. That, however, wasn't enough and she added more saying, "Get real, Stanley."

He barely managed to stammer out: "Of course for eternity. The tree is real. The heart is real. My love for you is real."

She pulled away before his tongue had the chance to form the letter O in the Of course and said, "You took me to see a carved up tree? God, when are you ever going to grow up?"

What he was hearing didn't make sense. First, she never called him, Stanley. Then she said, her words a cross between an order and a threat reminding him of his grandfather after the gin shoved aside another toast: "Take me home."

Before he realized, she was heading for the car at a pace between a jog and an all out sprint. Suddenly, she stopped, turned, put her hands on her hips and shouted, "Are you or aren't you coming?"

He stood like a marble statue waiting for pigeons to roost on his head, their white droppings decorating him.

"Now, Stupid," she ordered. "Not tomorrow!"

He was numb. A week earlier he had driven to the forest preserve on a whim, his mind always creating ways to show her how he loved her; to be creative in his words of love to her. This would be his all-time best; and old fashioned way like the lyrics to an equally old fashioned song. "The girl that I marry will have to be...." That's when he searched for the perfect tree for his monument to her; to announce to the world his love for her. He had carved a heart in the trunk of the maple using his

Boy Scout pocket knife, the one his parents had given him in grammar school. He had kept the blades sharp, the smaller more suited to obeying the artist's hand and that of a skilled surgeon as it left his loving scar, their intricate initials deep into the tree's flesh with all the care of a creative artisan. Both hearts, his and the maple's, were filled with his love for her. He knew she loved him. She had his gold class ring with the oval red stone, a gold block *W* in the middle, and the simulated gold ring guard that had reduced his number ten finger size into less than half so the ring would fit her slender finger. That was the second class ring he had given her. The first one she had taken off in the restroom of The Escape, a dressy restaurant they had gone to celebrate their going steady. The Escape was their special place. At least he thought it was. The first time there she had gone to the restroom and forgot the ring on the bathroom sink.

He had worn her class ring around his neck on a chain, receiving it the same day she did at the end of her junior year. Her ring was also gold, tiny in comparison to his. He couldn't afford a gold chain and bought what he could, being careful to wash the circular green outline that would develop around his neck once-a-week.

He stood staring at his masterpiece etched in the tree, eyes not blinking, a brain not comprehending and senses oblivious to the warm autumn air blowing across the grove. The more he stared at the carved heart, the more he began to feel like his original class ring disappearing from a bathroom sink. He finally blinked and turned around to see she was standing by the side of the car. He jogged across the dormant grass of the picnic grove toward the car void of feeling, not knowing what to say. She took a step out of the way as he opened the door for her, always the gentleman. He couldn't believe what he heard next.

Tears washed down her cheeks as she choked out: "Take me home and I never want to see you again."

He tried to talk to her as he drove, his questions getting only silence, her shoulders quivering. He felt as if his insides had evaporated.

"There's nothing to talk about," she finally said a block from where she lived, putting a chill on the weather that had been riding an unseasonably warm hump from October to November. She stared straight ahead as if she were riding in a crowded elevator.

"Why?" he asked, feeling his throat plug up. "What did I do? Please tell me? I won't do it again."

"You didn't do a thing," she said, her words sounding like she had just stabbed him with his own Boy Scout knife without opening a blade. "Stop acting like a big baby and trying to be perfect all the time," she continued, her words gouging out more chunks of his heart and discarding them on his surprise.

His words slowly transformed into frustrated pleas, but she just turned her head and looked out the passenger side window never saying a word. The car barely stopped in front of her parents' tiny two bedroom ranch house and her door popped open, her standing outside before the sound of the pop ended. She looked inside the car, his door just being opened as he tried to scoot out from behind the steering wheel, one leg in the car and one leg out.

"Don't bother," she said, as she stepped away from the car, turned and ran across the parkway lawn to the front entrance, the lower half of the screen to the storm door missing since before he met her.

Another plea was ready to depart his lips when she stopped and turned back to the car. "Tell your mom and dad hi for me."

A numb blink was his reply.

"And, Stanley," she said changing from polite to stern, issuing an order he wouldn't obey. "Please don't call me." Then she was gone.

Chapter 4

He ignored her last request. "Don't call me," he repeated dozens of times, the only person hearing him being him. His index finger almost wore out the numbers on the lone phone in his parent's house. She didn't budge from her last request, shunning his calls but he kept trying; listening to her mother making up excuses for her daughter; hearing the phone click after his respectful, "God morgon or God aftermiddag" depending on what time he called. After awhile, Annamargret Pearson politely said to Stan in her heavy Swedish accent, "My Johanna needs time."

He respected Johanna's mother's request, but he refused to let his *El B* go. Instead, he let go of everything else in his life. What little desire he possessed for living was funneled into creating his single page black book. That lone page received more care than the maple tree and took over his life. Wisps of his artistic creativity divided both sides of the page into tiny segments. Each segment consisted of his emotions in precise alphabetical order written in his version of Olde English script as if by the skilled hand of a monk and underlined in red ink. *Ache* and *Agony* led the list. *B* and *C* were left off because they conjured up derogatory remarks about females. *D* was there representing *Dejection, Despair,* and *Desperation.* He had inserted *Heartbreak* and *Hurt* and gave the first *H* several extra red underscores, his sad reminder that he was the reason she had slammed the door in his face. He let her get away. There was *Pain*, too much, and *Pleasure*, ranging from too little to, in his words, "Pleasure! What the hell is that?" The last word on his list was **R** representing *Rejection*. On the back inside cover was a neatly printed verse, a song he remembered as a little kid, sung for sad little kids. Now he was the sad, little kid singing his sad song to himself.

Nobody loves me. Everybody hates me. I'll guess I'll go eat worms.

Chapter 5

The memory of sitting in his car staring at the front door of her house where she had vanished from his life without looking back had taken forever to leave him, but it did; at least on the surface. Now he was looking at other doors; heavy glass ones constantly sliding back and forth; humanity appearing, facial expressions flashing messages like a collection of garish neon billboards. Hordes of people kept coming at him through the doors, almost too fast for him to sort out the one face he wasn't sure he wanted to see. He stood by the side of his car, one foot in and the other out, his arms propped on the car's roof, an instant replay of almost forty years earlier, his brain trying to make sense of what was going on. Frustrated, he kept asking, "Stanley, what's the matter with you?" Then angrily hearing the answer which he already knew, "You know you can't go back," echoing through his head along with honking horns, police whistles, brakes squeaking and engines revving. "Why are you even here?" His question was followed by an uncharacteristic Stan who never swore: "Stanley, you're a fuckin' moron." He knew that anger was the result of fear, even long entombed fear unearthed after decades. "What are you afraid of?" he asked. He had no answer for the question that got lost in the chilly wind blowing under the canopied Arrival Lanes as he tried to stay calm; fearing he was about to bolt; leaving her the way she had left him. He didn't have to answer his question. His mind had concocted her reply. There was a vision of her standing next to the maple tree, leaves on fire, her coldly telling him what she had once told him. "You're so immature." He smiled, remembering the words, now surprising himself by agreeing with her. "You were so right," he said softly, the sea of anonymous faces pouring out the terminal doors not hearing him and not caring if they did.

His eyes kept traveling along United's Arrival area, scanning, shifting waiting for the police to move him along, his car having already made the massive O'Hare loop around the cluster of terminals three times. He was characteristically early hoping that her plane would follow his lead. It didn't. They had originally talked on the phone about having her call the moment the plane landed and he would leave for the airport. Then, decades of insecure memories flooded over him filled with mistrust. "It'll be easier if I just meet you where I said," he told her over the phone just before her flight left from Boston's Logan International. "Walk across two lanes of cab, limo and bus traffic to the outside lane of the Arrival level," he had explained to her during the brief reassuring call.

He both cursed and laughed at the feeling of armored butterflies bouncing off the walls of his stomach acting like the German Panzer attacks he had heard as a small child; the stories coming from his Grandpa Zev, the gin in command. His grandfather, a baby faced teenager, frail in stature during World War II, had been recruited by the Belgium underground to spy on the Germans. His spying didn't last long. The Germans didn't hide their intentions; didn't wait for diplomatic, respectful, more humane terms of engagement agreed upon by combatants before attempting to slaughter one another. He watched the Panzer's unleash deafening, horrific cannon fire on the block of row houses; one of them his; the frustration of not being able to warn anyone of the pending devastation and doom numbing him. That day his grandfather began walking. He walked appearing as if he were in a trance, not quite a modern day version of a zombie. His entire being was on alert for anything or anyone who vaguely resembled a swastika or a Nazi. He traveled only at night; ate what he could pick, dig, scrounge or steal. There wasn't much. The Germans had taken what they could eat, wear or sell; sometimes taking women, raping and discarding what was left over. His sense of smell could pick up the aroma of a cigarette; the zombie altering his course. If a soldier on guard duty urinated, he could hear it. He heard the whispered conversation of the enemy understanding only snippets of German. Hunger, battling the elements and his high state of being alert was taking a toll on him. That's when he found himself in a small coastal town; saw fishing boats and flipped a coin. Heads or tails didn't matter. He stowed away on a rusted, foul smelling trawler headed for he knew not where, and didn't care, as long as it was away from Germans. The gagging stench of the garbage scow kept the Germans and their vicious dogs away. The German patrol boats avoided them. They had seen and smelled the mounds of putrid garbage way too often. The scow's routine never changed. This night the ship appeared later. The German sailor on watch couldn't be bothered; his face buried inside the collar of his heavy coat, more to block out the stench than protect him from the cold, damp air. His thoughts were on his girl back in Dusseldorf and he never saw the scow's lights get turned off and it disappearing in the opposite direction from where it came. Young Grandpa Zev crawled out from the garbage on another shore, a different one, in another country and still walking. Then he was on another boat; this one bigger and minus the stench. When the boat docked his young legs took aim for a place he heard his parents and relatives talk about; a place where his people lived; a Belgium area in a place called Chicago. He finally stopped walking when he found himself living with an aunt on the north side of Chicago and in class at St. Gregory's High School.

Stan had fought his own fight to stay alive by running, not walking, from the demons he had allowed to latch onto his heart, threatening to devour it along with his soul. No one could ever know how he felt buried under the oppressive page of his black book so long ago, existing at best, living for a hope, wanting to eat those worms in that kid's song that went, *"Big fat juicy ones; Tiny, squirmy, squiggly ones."*

For too many years after Johanna had left him, Stan carried the cross of immaturity she had bequeathed to him. He dropped out of college, drank too much, and didn't care at times that he might end up owning his own five gallon crock and brewing gin. Two days after an agonizing New Year's Eve alone listening to his Tony Bennett albums, and specifically the one song about Joanna once loving him, that love without an "h" in her name, he enlisted in the Air Force. He spent almost two years at the Misawa Air Force Base in the north of Japan trying to intercept the Russian Bear's messages and deciphering what Ivan was planning on doing to the United States and other countries with the Iron Curtain it had hung. Stan, for the most part, served his country as a "Ditty Bop" and stayed away from the local bars in the small mud hole of a town with open sewers and inhabited primarily by fisherman and farmers. Joining the fishermen and farmers was a large population of cocktail waitresses working the local bars in Misawa that catered to the military personnel. They did their own form of angling and harvesting. Then Stan met Kimiko Tamaka in the PX. She was a house girl for one of the big brass, one of a very few officers who had his family shipped over to Japan. Stan suddenly forgot about Johanna. He forgot about the devastation of her jilting him. There was no Indian summer north of Mount Fujiyama. April in Paris was snowed under by cherry blossoms. Almond eyes and broken English had him feeling what his black book wouldn't let him feel. He found himself in what he thought was love with Kimi, as he called her. Their romance was a series of one well spaced secret and one well spaced rendezvous after another. The big brass paid Kimiko well to take care of his two children and fraternization with any of his men was off limits. The main part of her job was to literally wait on, and look out after, his prudish crusading wife with the Petunia Pig face who hated being stuck in what she had referred to as a cesspool house of ill-repute inhabited by ugly little people who the atom bomb had missed. She was livid at the sight of American boys, Air Force boys, her husband's boys, fraternizing with, as she referred to the female Japanese citizens, "those hideous looking Asian harlots with buck teeth."

Stan also gave money to Kimi for her family when he went to see her on her day off. He had met her parents, both of them farmers who worked a small plot of land that barely fed them. He even shared a nervous hot bath with them. The first time he went to get into the steaming tub with a naked Kimi and her equally naked parents and two younger sisters, he wanted to wear his GI issued underwear. A collective shaking of smiling heads and pointing of index fingers in the direction of his Air Force issue boxer shorts put an end to his nervousness. Marriage soon crept into his mind about the time he was to be transferred back home to be discharged. He had never hugged another human being with so much emotional silence, not even Johanna. There were her tears and his playfully flicking her on the tip of her doll-like nose with the curled up big knuckle of his right index finger the way he had done from almost the moment they met; the way he used to do to Johanna. He had no tears, not on the outside like hers. His were still buried inside, all used up, dried up, from long ago. Then they both said, "Sayonara." He told her that he would call her the moment he got home. They vowed to write to each other every day until the red tape could be cut away for her to come to the United States. "You'll love my parents," he assured her. "Just the way I love Mama-san and Papa-san." He never did call and she never did write.

Chapter 6

After he was discharged he studied art at Chicago's Art Institute. His artistic talents were unlimited. At one time back when he had first started drawing, he wanted to do a portrait of Johanna; that was after she had become *El B*. She had turned him down without realizing how good of an artist he was. He didn't recognize his talent then, his mind clogged with fantasies and wanting to draw her like so many pictures of the pin-up girls he had seen as a young boy. He had peaked at every pointed breast, covered or not; at every teasing smile surrounded by a halo of auburn, blond, brunette, henna, red or whatever colored hair framed a pretty face. He stole glances at everything from a calendar in his father's garage to magazines left open by careless uncles. Doing an oil painting of *El B* as she posed in the nude was his wildest fantasy. Her nude form never did get transferred to his canvas in oils. Several others did, professional models posing in art class and minus all possible fantasies. Kimiko had disappeared from his life like the last puff of a cigarette, one of many he went through during a normal twenty four hour shift a head set his only other companion.

He had reluctantly tossed out the memories depicted in the color slides he had taken of Kimiko. There were pictures of her as a pin-up along with one of his favorites, her in an ornate embroidered kimono. He had taken roll upon roll of film, all developed and printed on the base by an airman first class that had set up his own version of a budding pornography business. There were pictures of Kimiko minus her kimono; pictures of her with no dress of any kind, wearing no nothing. Thanks to his 35 mm's automatic shutter release and a tripod, there were provocative pictures of them making love. He had burned them all. As the photographs curled up into charred ashes, his memories of Kimiko followed the wisps of smoke curling up, thinning out and vanishing into the air.

Stan had cleaned up his ashes and found himself as a regular at way too many bars. All of the customers knew and liked him, especially the women. He had so much female companionship that he had joked about it to himself, apologizing secretly to Tony Bennett for taking the words to one of his older popular hits and singing, "I know I'd go from bags to bitches." When he would meet someone who grabbed him by more than his private parts, someone with a sincere heart and a face to match, he would retreat and become as affectionate as a snail. Snug and secure in his hiding place, he'd revisit Tony Bennett and recite the words to one of Tony's first songs, a song from before Stan was born, "Good-bye, I hate to see you go, but have a good time." He never would finish the song, the lyrics getting caught in his throat. Staying snug and secure also meant making telephone calls to keep him that way. For whatever reasons, his messages never seemed to register and the faces and sincere hearts kept calling him. He was still the gentleman, listening; the consummate master of small talk ending the conversation with his memorized lie so polite that the caller didn't realize she was history. He was always cheery and upbeat putting a final period on the small talk with, "Tell you what, give me a chance to get out from under my mountain of charcoal, oil and water colors and we'll go out to dinner Saturday; some place special," he would suggest, then interjecting a pause. "How does Don the Beachcomber's sound?" He sounded as if the reservation had already been made. There was a quick goodbye with the voice at the other end of the line unable to see the ball point pen in his hand, the button end coated with teeth marks as it created another unemotional line through a name; a hair color being eradicated and no black dots being formed. Then, before he could remove his hand from the phone and close his red book, *El B* would be standing in front of him, laughing and teasing, "Hey, immature little boy, would you like to eat my worms?" Then his mountain of charcoal, oil and water colors would come crashing down on him and *El B* would vanish after saying something related like, "My worms are juicier than those at Don the Beachcomber's."

* * * * *

Once, he would have done anything to get Johanna back and become the *B's* again. He missed coming up for air in the back seat at the drive-in movie, gasping, his lungs quivering for air, especially in the beginning, at the start of the end. Even after Kimiko and the others, he was always telling *El B's* vision, especially if he were drunk, the same slurring vow, "I'll always love you, Johanna." Alcohol even had him begging at times. She would toss her head back and laugh, then swallow one of the worms and fade out. "Why," he would always ask? "What did I do?" Then, one day, he forgot to ask and didn't ask again until his wife had died and then his mother followed.

Chapter 7

The memory of Johanna Pearson was unearthed shortly after his mother's funeral both jolting his heart and returning feelings to him he had thought were gone forever. Stan had married the only non one-night stand he met after his line of Tony Bennett cast-offs. He had seen Dee for the first time at a Halloween costume party thrown by two gay art students and classmates of his who owned a condo on the Gold Coast overlooking Oak Street Beach. Stan and Dee hit it off, her sense of humor and a love of British comedies a tonic for him. "Hi," she said to him from behind an umbrella the first time they met, "I'm Mary Poppins and I'm a Junkie." They dated, their dates about as old fashioned as old fashioned dates could get. There were hand-in-hand walks through Lincoln Park that included multiple visits to the zoo, the seals being their favorite stop where Dee's imitations made his head ache from laughing. They strolled the Magnificent Mile pretending to spend money they didn't have in all of the top-of-line status shops. He even suggested going on a picnic to the Forest Preserves. He later told her why. She made faces at him, packed a picnic basket and took him by the hand and led him to the postage stamp size backyard of the apartment building where she lived. Her studio apartment was on the third floor. There was a blanket spread on the lawn that was more dandelions than grass. Peanut butter and jelly sandwiches made up lunch along with a pitcher of frozen daiquiris, the pitcher having a small leak that made their sandwiches soggy. After, they had trudged up the three flights of wooden stairs at the back of the building and almost made love in her tiny kitchenette. Dee had straddled him on one of her two folding card chairs that was stenciled across the back in a faded white, *Madonna High School*. They were both gasping when she slid off his lap, clothing still intact and eyes knowing that wouldn't be the case if there was a second time. There was a second time, but that was after their wedding where she wore white.

Stan and Dee raised three daughters and had a life with normal ups and downs and one major challenge, getting their youngest daughter through the teen years. He had genuinely loved Dee and honored his vows. Then, after the kids had enrolled them in the ranks of empty nesters, Dee suffered an aneurism. She was at the Old Orchard Shopping Center in Saks Fifth Avenue, her favorite store, camped at the perfume counter. There was a test spray of some new exotic essence on her wrist, a whiff, and he was a widower. The shock had barely worn off when he found himself tending to his mother's meager estate. That's when *El B* surfaced.

Chapter 8

Stan was cleaning up his mother's tiny one bedroom apartment in the retirement home, tossing out what little remained from her life, saving only a few cherished belongings, knickknacks and such, the ones she hadn't broken in fits of her own despair. Curious, he flipped open the cover of her old, chipped sewing box, an ornate carved mahogany treasure belonging to her grandmother. She had the box since before he was born. There, among a collection of ageless buttons, he saw it and knew right away that it was *El B's* high school ring. He carefully, almost with as much tenderness as he used to flick Kimiko's nose, examined the ring like a jeweler peering at a gem through his eye glass. There was her school's name, Riverside-Brookfield High School and, her initials, JDP engraved inside the tiny gold circle. He tried it on his little finger. The fit was even tighter now barely clearing his finger nail. His thumb and forefinger caressed the ring and he asked aloud: "Ma, how did you get this?" His mind began racing, ignoring the caution flags. "I wonder if . . ."

Several nervous phone calls ended in frustration with him talking to himself even more. "You'd sure make a rotten detective." He kept reminding himself he was doing something nice even after calls to the high school and to Eastern Illinois University where he had heard she had gone to school proved fruitless. He tried Northern, Western and Southern Illinois as well; even Illinois College and Northwestern. No one was giving out information about alums, former students or employees regardless of the reason. He was being totally unselfish, at least he was telling himself that, but his self wasn't buying his rationale just the way the schools kept their records away from prying eyes. "Heck," he thought, "she'd surely like the ring. Maybe she could give it to one of her kids, if she were still alive." His thoughts quickly went back to Dee and the shock of that day. He had unloaded both their high school memorabilia on their adult children. He recalled hearing that *El B* had a daughter, but that was twenty five years ago, maybe thirty. "Was it that long ago?" he asked himself. Then seeing images of him as a teenager in love carving his artistic heart into the innocent maple tree. Then not knowing why he said what he said next, he muttered to the maple tree, "I really didn't mean to hurt you with my Boy Scout knife."

* * * * *

His cousin, Ziggy the cop, had finally located her in Cambridge, Massachusetts, living in a renovated Victorian not too far from Harvard Square. The computer had done the work, scanning birth dates and driver's license records. Stan always had trouble remembering the birthdays of his children, even Dee's and his mother's, but never *El B's*. He could even rattle off her old telephone number, "LY3-4975," he said aloud, grinning, proud of his accomplishment, wondering why his mind hadn't let that remnant drift away.

"Well, I got two possibles," his cousin had said to him over the phone, sounding like a pleased cop after bagging his prey. "One's five foot seven and weighs a hundred and twenty. The other's a blonde, same birth date. There was a pause and then the sound of his cousin blowing his nose as if he were using the phone's mouth piece for a handkerchief. "Looks here like Blondie has Goodyear painted on her ass and flies over the Super Bowl for her livelihood."

Stan knew Johanna wasn't Miss Goodyear. She couldn't have changed he thought. His cousin had given him her exact height and weight from when she was a senior in high school. She would never let herself get out of shape he told himself. Adding, "There might be a line or a wrinkle or two above the neck, but she'll fight gravity to the grave before she gives up her shape.

When they met it had been love at first sight for Stan and Johanna. She became Stan's fair lady and the street where she lived became his second address. His love embraced even her parents and older sister, Gale who was twenty two and divorced. Gale would always quiz them as to what took place on their dates; her questions always bordering on the risqué to the downright suggestive with more than sexual overtones. It was Gale who had nicknamed them both.

"At the drive-in," Gale blurted out amazed as the three of them sat in the tiny living room of the Pearson house. "You two actually watched the movie at a drive-in?" She looked at Stan shaking her head in disbelief. "Besides, where on earth did you find a drive-in movie that's open?"

Stan nodded over his shoulder. "Somewhere out that direction in one of those out of the way suburbs where Moses lost his sandals," he said.

Gale's attention turned back to Johanna. The quiz was about to follow. "Dearest younger sister," she started, right eyebrow cocked like a jungle cat ready to pounce, "why do you dislike this poor guy so much?"

"Where did you ever get that idea?" Johanna asked, knowing that her sister was notorious for her teasing, sometimes not knowing when to draw the line. Playful to Gale wasn't always funny to Johanna and, as she knew, not to her sister's ex-husband who tired of his wife flirting with his best friend. The best friend had taken it as more than flirting and ended up no longer being a best friend; Gale no longer being a wife. Johanna barely managed to squeeze out an, "Why would you think going to a drive-in means I hate Stan?"

"Because he's a guy and guys, like some gals I know, don't always have the willpower to draw the line."

Stan turned away. He knew all about drawing the line. His was etched in granite. He didn't like his line, but he respected it the way he respected Johanna.

Johanna began to exhibit a combination blush and flush of anger and said, "Gale, change the subject."

Gale knew her sister was upset with her. She flashed a big smile that exposed her two front teeth that had no space between them making her look as if she had one big upper tooth. "Besides, men can turn into real animals when you least expect." Her smile grew wider. "With your looks and body I bet you could turn this guy into a real beast with or without a drive-in movie."

Stan knew Gale was right. Johanna had a magnificent body complete with ample hips that had a perfect contour and breasts that attracted stares, gawks, gapes and second looks; the looks often accompanied by sound effects.

Gale grinned on. "Stan, I think from now on I'm going to call you El Beasto," she said all of her teeth exposed. "And, so you don't feel excluded, little sister, I think you should be called

El Breasto."

The names had stuck; the Beast and the Breast, shortened to *El B*, together and forever more. Then a maple tree and a confused, frightened teen-age girl sent forever into the ever after and Stan could have cared less about getting past nineteen.

* * * * *

Stan wasn't in his late teens now. He had grudgingly emerged from that stage of his life scarred, scared and skeptical. Now, as he slowed down his car for the fourth time in front of the span of United's arrival doors, he began the scanning process again, his senses heightened the way they were decades ago when he would sit in a zone for hours as a "Ditty Bop." His car edged to the curb of the outside lane in front of Terminal One. This time he kept both of his feet on the edge of the frame using the car as a boost to get extra height, wanting a better view and wondering aloud, "Oh, crap, maybe she's at another door." He could see the sliding doors in front of him as well as those to his far right and left. His nervous, apprehensive eyes sifted through the never-ending line of passengers heading for him. She wasn't one of them. He knew he had told her about the outside passenger car lane or had he. "Damn," he said aloud again, and then his mind erupted. "Gosh darn it, Ma," he muttered, "you better be right." Her prophecy was still tattooed on his teen-aged brain.

"If it's meant to be, it will be," she had said to him when she could no longer tolerated seeing her son's long face with the weight of a forlorn look dragging the corners of his mouth down to where they rested on his chest. Then she added, sounding like Johanna's mother, "Time will tell. It might take a while, but if it's meant to be, it will be."

Stan's father wasn't as philosophical as Stan's mother, no pearls on his strand of words. "Women are like the CTA bus," he said without looking up from the copy of the Sun-Times he was reading. "They come along right on schedule," he continued, his description of Johanna angering his son. "You get on, pay your fare and, if you don't like the ride, you get off at the next stop."

Before Stan could vent, his father continued.

"Son, you'll know when you've found the right bus," he continued with a slight trace of a smile. "Your mother and I paid our fares years ago and we've enjoyed the ride ever since."

Stan's other grandfather his dad's dad was a man of few words, none of them philosophical, all dictatorial. He was known simply and respectfully as, Grandpa; "Gramps" to Stan and, like his Grandpa Zev, Stan idolized the man and was in awe of his accomplishments in life. He also feared him but didn't know why. Gramps was short in stature, shorter even than Grandpa Zev and never had to flee for his life from German soldiers and tanks. This grandfather's life saw him having to leave school in the eighth grade to find work and help a widowed mother and six younger brothers and sisters survive. Whatever money he earned, sometimes mere pennies, went to his mother. He was like Stan's Boy Scout knife: trustworthy, loyal and always on hand. He also organized the best floating crap games on the near northwest side of Chicago of which he took a fair fee for his efforts of keeping the games police free. Gramps also became a trusted gopher for the alderman of his ward. He did anything. If flyers needed delivering, he delivered. If campaign signs needed posting, he posted the signs; tearing down those of the opposition. His loyalty was rewarded and he found himself as an assistant precinct captain. Soon the term assistant vanished and he was the sole captain of his precinct. He knocked on every door, talked to every voter and helped those who couldn't help themselves even though his mother needed more help than the others. When he was old enough he found himself appointed to some nondescript political position that paid real money. He continued to do what it took and even more to help his mother. Soon he was slated as a candidate for a real political position. He was back to knocking on doors. Doorbells were rung and hands were shook. Someone even tore down some his posters. Gramps discovered real estate. Then he discovered insurance. He got into banking. His mother, brothers and sisters no longer wanted. Mother was comfortable and secure; his brothers and sisters were married with families and had careers of their own. Things couldn't be better. What Gramps didn't know was that his heart could have been better.

* * * * *

Stan thought a lot about Gramps after Johanna left him. He thought about how his life would have been if Gramps' own heart hadn't left him; if maybe Gramps might have had some words of wisdom to help him through his turmoil. The more he thought, the more he remembered that Gramps was a man who had one real pearl of wisdom to share, that being: "God only helps those who help themselves." That little jewel of philosophy had been literally dumped on Stan by Gramps via a fish.

What Stan remembered most about Gramps was a fishing trip to Canada with his father, grandparents, his aunt and uncle and his cousin, Ginger. His mother had stayed behind with his two sisters and a baby brother. The only thing his mother liked about fishing was eating the final product. It was during that fishing trip when Stan thought his boyhood world had collapsed. "It's not fair, Gramps" he had said respectfully, to the man who was a head shorter than Stan.

"Life isn't always fair," Gramps had said back, while Stan's father looked on from the middle seat of the long, wide, faded red aluminum boat they had been fishing from. The splashes and swirls from the biggest fish he had ever seen had disappeared. That same fish, earlier, had been responsible for the splashes and swirls that pulled the fishing rod from Stan's hands with a warning about making him eat worms in the future. He was still numb from the loss and unable to comprehend what had happened. His father and grandfather weren't. They knew.

Chapter 9

Stan's life had been more than fair before then, before love; back when he was just stepping into the world of a teenager. It had been Gramps' suggestion. "Bring the kid," he remembered hearing his grandfather tell his dad. "Consider it my graduation present to him from eighth grade." He recalled how Gramps had paused and looked at him with eyes that were both envious and sad. "At least I can give you what I never had."

His dad had accompanied Stan, The Kid as he was referred to by adult family members, on a fishing trip to Canada; Kenora, Ontario was the town and Red Indian Lodge on Lake of the Woods was the place. They rode on the train to Kenora, Ontario. He thought he heard his dad tell his grandfather that they would be taking the Northwestern out of a station in downtown Chicago. He and his dad were going to sleep in a Pullman car berth from Chicago to St. Paul or Minneapolis. He didn't really remember. The train station was grimy, the grainy black veneer of coal filth still coating a portion of his brain. He recalled how antsy he was to get where they were going. They waited sitting on a stained varnish bench that had seen too many bodies during and after World War II. His father chewed on a cigar, intermittently jumping up from the dingy bench like an arthritic jack-in-the-box pacing the floor of the grey, depressing terminal. He listened and watched for their track number and the next train that would take them to some other place called, Winnipeg. His dad would sit back down with a grunt knowing that the train trip was far from over. At the end, he and his dad would meet the rest of the family at the resort, a place that had the word, Indian in its name.

Stan hoped his cousin, Ginger, who was two years older and had threatened to run away from home if she had to go to Canada on a fishing trip, would not ruin his graduation present. To Stan, Ginger was a spoiled brat.

He and his dad had left what he heard referred to as the "Twin Cities" and were riding on another train; this one the Canadian National. He was sitting next to his dad in the dining car, sharing a table with a woman who had red hair in tight curls. She also had a swatch of freckles speckling her nose and her right cheek and she wore orange lipstick. He could see a speck of mayonnaise on the corner of her mouth from the chicken salad she was eating and tried not to stare as he waited and wondered when she ever planned to wipe her mouth. She ate slow, taking small bites, chewing what seemed to be forever to him while she looked at his dad, talking, her eyes seeming to say something else, while his dad politely listened. He couldn't see his dad's eyes.

They finally arrived in a place the conductor hollered out as, "Kenora!" They were met by a strange looking old man who had a face that resembled Stan's cracked leather baseball mitt. He wore a military style jacket complete with several rows of award ribbons, their colors faded. The old man greeted them with a stern expression and pointed to a rusted station wagon with wooden sides. "Put your things there," the man said, and pointed.

"Red Indian Lodge?" his father had asked.

The strange looking old man's head went up and down once and what resembled a grunt and a burp came from his mouth. He gave another nod in the direction of station wagon with the intriguing wooden sides.

Stan would never forget the ride. In seconds they left what little civilization was situated around the oblong frame train station with the single word, Kenora painted in a faded white at each end, to driving along a black top road and entering a cavern of what he learned were majestic Norway Red Pine trees. All he knew then was that the inside of the station wagon was dirtier than the train station in the Twin Cities and that the tears in the upholstery outnumbered the non-tears by four to one. He also heard his father ask their driver, "You're taking us to Red Indian Lodge on Whitefish Bay, Lake of the Woods, right?" There was another single nod and a combination grunt and burp. Then the driver introduced himself by saying, "Me Charlie Two Feathers. I'm a Sioux and I was a spy for the British government during World War II."

Hearing that the driver was both an Indian and a former spy kept Stan's interest boiling, but that didn't last long as the steaming pot turned into a stagnant container of water as the man known as Charlie Two Feathers never said another word. What seemed like a boring eternity to him ended when the station wagon came to screeching stop in front of a poorly painted totem pole. The totem pole stood on a slight angle leaning forward in front of a large stone and log building that he swore had a tree growing out of the middle of the roof. He shortly learned that what he thought he saw was actually a tree growing through the center of a building that was the main lodge of the resort.

"Welcome," said the driver, who then introduced himself again. "Me Charlie Two Feathers." He proceeded to explain to his two passengers that he was now a Seneca Chief but still a spy for the English in a new war, this one in a place called Korea. His dad later learned that Charlie had been knocked silly by a railroad switch handle that caught him above the left ear when he was stumbling back to the reservation one night. He had been following the train track on that sub-zero night after too much to drink in town. Charlie somehow got his tribes scrambled along with his brains. He was a member of the Cree and his career as a spy for the King actually began in 1950, but only in his mind.

Stan and his dad stayed in the smallest bedroom of a three-bedroom log cabin, the bedroom the same size as their bed. The cramped quarters didn't please his father who made Stan crawl over the sagging mattress where he found himself wedged against the drafty cabin wall and his father. The cabin had uneven field stone front stairs that wrecked havoc on his grandmother's arthritic legs causing her to spout out her frustration and pain in her two favorite Polish condemnations: "Jezus Maryja" she would grimace. That was followed by, "Matka Boska." Then his grandmother would hobble on, her bow legs making her five foot two frame more like two foot five.

The walls and ceiling of the cabin were knotty pine tongue and groove boards, a very subdued luster still showing off like a once sexy movie star finding that make-up doesn't work magic anymore. The furniture was faded, had a musty aroma that he got used to and seemed to be stuffed with the same field stones that were used on the front stairs. His grandparents had one bedroom; his aunt, uncle and Ginger had the largest of the three bedrooms; theirs had a private bath as did his grandparent's room. He and his dad were minus the luxury of a private bathroom theirs was down the hall via a trip through what appeared to be a kitchen. As Stan's father remarked after their first night of sleeping in the cabin, "That goddamned bed must've belonged to Chief Scrambled Brains. He probably used it to insulate the floor of his teepee."

Stan didn't care and, as he said to Ginger before going to bed that first night, "This place is kind of cool, don't you think?"

Ginger made a face, the epitome of disgust, and informed him, "I'm running away from here tonight and taking the train back to Chicago."

Stan, taken back, replied, "Tonight? Gee, you just got here." He paused and looked out the window over the huge lake and the most incredible sunset he had ever seen and asked, "But, what are you going to do when a moose or even worse, a bear comes out of the woods."

Ginger joined all of them in the lodge for breakfast the next morning. She stared at her orange juice sullen faced, rebellious, hating every second of her life and vowing to eradicate Canada from her memory.

There were times Stan questioned why he considered this grandfather as his idol as well as Grandpa Zev. He feared him. That wasn't the case with Grandpa Zev who always made him laugh with his antics. Gramps' name, Wladyslaw was enough to give him nightmares about Count Dracula, Frankenstein and the Wolfman. Yet, Gramps sat on Stan's altar alongside Grandpa Zev. He had total respect for him, possibly because his name meant powerful warrior even though he didn't look powerful, not with a belly that hung over his belt and jowls that jiggled back and forth when he walked or talked. Unlike all of his relatives who yelled when they talked, Gramps was soft spoken, his voice belonging to any of an army of radio disk jockeys playing the top songs from "Your Hit Parade." His grandfather's eyes were his Achilles Heel, changing from sensitive, comforting blue to shooting out bolts of lightning when he was upset. Stan rarely saw the upset side of him. Most times Gramps was pleasant, almost friendly to him, but never a pal or a buddy. He was Grandpa and Stan was the first born grandson in the family; the heir apparent and he had no idea he was being groomed to pick up where his grandfather one day would eventually leave off. Patriarch was not in Stan's vocabulary.

Gramps had amassed a small fortune by lending money to those who were of his ethnic heritage and had been turned down by every legitimate lending institution in the State of Illinois.

When Stan wasn't with his grandfather and uncle fishing from a boat with Charlie Two Feathers as their guide, he humored himself by watching his grandfather chain smoke English Ovals, and his dad and uncle remove the smelly cigar butts growing from the corners of their mouths only long enough to eat and sleep. In the evening he watched the parade of nicotine continue while his aunt and grandmother sat in front of a potbellied stove in the bleak living room wrapped in shawls even though it was mid-June. They knitted, their fingers flying as they whispered non-stop in their native Polish tongue. They hadn't smiled since arriving at the lodge.

Stan played War with Ginger who had suddenly thought

Canada had possibilities after she saw the family from Tennessee in the next cabin. They had a son who was going to play football for the University of Tennessee Volunteers that fall as a freshman. Orange suddenly became Ginger's favorite color and, in between deals, she would jump up and rummage through her clothes looking for anything that resembled Tennessee colors. She also threw a small tantrum after visiting the resort's main lodge. The pine log building with a Red Pine growing through the lodge's ceiling, had several book shelves on either side of a field stone fireplace that was so wide both Ginger and Stan could stand in it. The book shelves were jammed with old, hard cover books. Ginger returned to the cabin one evening after dinner complaining to her parents and anyone else who would listen. "Can you believe this place doesn't have a single book on Tennessee or the Civil War?" she started out, her words coated with a new found southern accent. "What kind of place did y'all bring little ol' me to?" she had asked, fuming. "Heavens, are Canadian people that ignorant that they don't have a thing to read about Knoxville?" Then her father told her to shut up and added, "Stop talking like a dumb hillbilly."

Her grandmother said something in Polish that he later learned had something to do with dog's blood. That made no sense to him what-so-ever.

Along with playing cards with Ginger in the evening, Stan fantasized about what the next day would bring when their fishing boat headed out on the hundred mile long lake. Would he catch a fish the size of those that adorned the walls of the lodge? His next thought was, "What would I do if I did get a big one on my line?" Not once did Stan complain and say,

"There's nothing to do." He knew better. When Ginger was throwing one of her snits he still had a deck of cards and the game of Solitaire to give him a break from his fantasies. His grandmother understood telling him how he could go through the deck as many times as he could by flipping over three cards at a time or going through it once, one card at a time. In the morning, while waiting to brush his teeth, he was told by his grandfather to eat a hearty breakfast. "If the fish are biting," his grandfather stated, "we won't be comin' in until dinner. Stan didn't have time to think about biting fish when he heard his grandfather warn: "And, don't forget to bring that old, empty coffee can. "We ain't going into shore if you have to take a leak."

Chapter 10

From the very beginning, after getting out of the station wagon, he was in awe of the size of the lake, even though he had seen only a portion of it from the resort's boat dock jutting out into Whitefish Bay. The one thing that stuck in his mind years later about the trip, even after Johanna, was the afternoon where his grandfather taught him a lesson about life not being fair.

The instigator had been a fish. To Stan, it was the Moby Dick of Lake of the Woods; bigger than Ahab's white whale. Now, decades later, Stan could close his eyes and see the True Temper steel fishing rod Gramps had let him use being bent into a crying horseshoe. Stan was too excited to care about the rod breaking. His heart almost stopped when the fish leapt out of the water mirroring the arc in the rod before landing in a splash so loud that he never knew water could make such a noise. It was then that the reel handle squirted from his hand; the handle spinning backwards; the black braided line buzzing into an instant bird's nest that made his heart stop. His heart kicked in again as he grabbed at the reel handle, missing it. A second try resulted in his choking it. He began cranking, the line coming in, crushing the bird's nest. The fish emerged again from under a patch of tranquil, green lily pads, the submerged eyes glaring. Before Stan could blink the angry eyes and a mouth full of jagged tent peg shaped teeth were replaced by a tail the size of the coal shovel his father used to stoke their furnace at home. The shovel wasted no time dousing him with what he thought had to be half the lake. Hanging on to the groaning fishing rod with one hand and trying to wipe lake water out of his eyes he saw the mouth full of teeth coming at him. This time the tent pegs had turned into flashing razor blades poised to take off both of his hands at the elbows. The angry green goliath swirled, defying Stan, sneering at him.

His father, frustrated with Charlie Two Feathers who sat giggling, grabbed the oars from the Indian. As he swung the oars and tried to switch oar locks, one of the oars hit Charlie Two Feathers with a glancing blow across his head. Charlie just giggled. Frustrated, Stan's father pushed and pulled on alternate oars, trying to turn the boat while shouting out two sets of orders. He barked one set to his son shouting: "Don't let him go under the boat!" In his next breath he zeroed in on Charlie. "Stop giggling like a hyena and help the kid!"

The others, including Ginger, were fishing from a larger cabin cruiser and being guided by a young strapping lad called, Ray Eagle. Charlie Two Feathers boasted that Ray was his son. He wasn't. Ray, upon hearing Charlie's introduction, simply put his right index finger up to his right temple and rotated it.

The cabin cruiser was more comfortable for his grandmother and aunt, Ginger opting to sun bath and think about Judd, her Tennessee Volunteer dreamboat. Stan's grandfather had joined the three women and fished from the cabin cruiser. He was catching skinny Northern Pike on almost every other cast, but wasn't happy knowing that the Ontario fish limit had him tossing every fish back in the water. The cabin cruiser rental fee galled his grandfather even more. He had enough money to buy an armada of such boats, but he was going to do his best to make the ladies, who weren't fishing, smile. Instead, they chatted, knitted and pretended to sulk until the excitement started with Stan. Soon, they too were shouting their encouragement. Ginger could have cared less and sat looking back in the direction of where she thought the resort was and wondering what it would be like to live in Knoxville.

Gramps exhibited his own form of encouragement by shouting to his grandson, "Don't drop the goddamned rod in the drink!"

Stan barely heard his grandfather's warning skipping across Lake of the Woods buried in an echo or his dad's instructions. One nervous hand choked the rod's small, tapered cork grip situated just in front of the tangled reel. His other nervous hand clamped on the reel handle. He yanked and cranked. He pulled and groaned. He heard his father's repetitious warning, "Keep a tight line. Reel, for chrissake." That was followed by an embellished warning and new echo from Gramps, "Goddammit, Kid, don't drop the sumbitchin' rod into the lake."

Stan reached back, finding some hidden strength, and yanked as hard as he could. His clenched hand slipped from the reel again and then the rod slipped. He felt himself being propelled backwards, his legs pointing toward the clear sky as his head hit the bottom of the aluminum boat with an echoing thunk. "The rod!" he heard his grandfather scream. "Save the goddamn rod!"

"Screw the rod, Pa," his father bellowed. "Get the goddamn fish in the boat, Kid."

The rod was between his legs now and all he could see was sky along with a flash of lightening and several shooting stars.

He groped for the rod and scrambled to get upright. His fingers felt the line on the bottom of the boat and he strangled it, yanking. The line zipped through his hands, cutting them, bringing blood. He felt the burning pain as the lightning and shooting stars vanished. The line jumped free. He grimaced and pawed at the rod handle trying to get a grip. Now, kneeling in the bottom of the boat, he tried to ignore his bleeding hand. "Got you," he said, through clenched teeth, grabbing the rod and forcing the butt into his stomach. He yanked the rod again, harder, and caught himself from falling backward by rocking forward on his knees. The reel handle was barely moving as he forced the snarled line on the spool. The rod was straight. He looked at his dad. "I got 'em! I got 'em!" The tangled line kept building up on the reel. "I got you now," he said, bracing himself for what he knew would be more than a life or death showdown. Instead, the end of the line slithered limply from the water. There was no fish. No hook. No nothing.

He looked back and forth at the line and his dad not believing. Then he looked at the limp, dangling line minus his metal leader and hook with the bright brass spinner. "It's not fair, Dad," he said, not believing. "He got away." He couldn't believe how empty he felt. He was beyond defeated.

His dad seemed different, more subdued, a sympathetic look in his eyes, saying to him, "Son, dip those hands of yours in the lake and wash off that blood." He nodded toward the side of the boat. "It might sting," he warned his voice full of compassion. Then, in a whisper, he said, "Don't let your aunt and grandmother think you're hurt. Your grandfather's in enough hot water for bringing those two up here. All they have to see is you with some cut fingers and he'll find himself tossed in the lake with our boat anchor around his neck."

The water was cold and Stan didn't feel much of a sting. He wasn't feeling much of anything except trying to figure out what had just happened.

"Son," he heard his father say, as Stan removed his dripping hands from the lake, "that's what's known as the one that got away." Stan felt his father gently take the rod from him. "Let's see what we can do about this mess of tangled line before your grandfather sees it," he said smiling.

He watched as his dad started picking at the bird's nest while continuing with, "Don't worry, Son, there's a lot more fish where that came from." He looked up and nodded at Stan's hands. "How are the hands feeling?"

Choking back his tears, "They're okay, Dad," he said, feeling a lump jammed in his throat. "That fish was mine."

His uncle didn't sound very sympathetic when he said, "Sometimes you get the lunker and sometimes the lunker gets you."

His dad continued to pick at the menagerie of tangled line. "Son, it just wasn't meant to be."

He watched his father's fingers picking, pulling, poking and prodding at the ball of line that seemed to be getting smaller. Then he saw the party boat with Ray Eagle come along side, the larger boats bow hitting them broadside with a boat rocking bounce. He looked at his grandfather and said, "It's not fair, Gramps."

Gramps reached across and took the rod and tangled reel from his dad. "Mmmm," he grunted softly, and began pulling a long length of line free from the reel. That seemed to please him even though the reel stopped moving. "Kid," Gramps said, staying on his quest, "life isn't always fair. Sometimes Lady Luck deals you a bad hand."

"Your grandfather's right," his uncle said, adding to the remarks as his eyes focused on the tangled line sprouting out from the reel. "Just remember that you can only blame bad luck once in a while." He pointed at Stan. "The rest of the time you make your own luck because Lady Luck, well, Lady Luck works that way." His uncle gave him a faint smile. "Kid," he started out and then paused... "You'll find that women are like that," he continued with a wink. "You never know what they're going to do."

"What's Lady Luck got to do with my fish getting away?" asked Stan getting the feeling that his father, grandfather and uncle didn't know how he was feeling.

"Everything and nothing," he remembered his father saying. Then he heard his grandfather, "Besides, there are plenty more fish where that one came from." Then his father took his eyes off the untangled line Gramps was working on and said, "Lady Luck might have you catch that same fish again. Who knows? One thing's for sure. He's still swimming around out there."

None of what had happened that day mattered or made sense to him. His fish had gotten away.

* * * * *

A little over five years later, nothing mattered or made sense when *El B* said her goodbye to him in a voice so cold he could feel the fishing line slide through his fingers wanting to draw blood. The problem was his blood had turned to ice and he had no way of comprehending her final words. "I hope we can still be friends, but don't ever call me again."

* * * * *

Lady Luck didn't have a thing to do with Johanna slamming the door on his love for her. What bothered him the most was that she never told him whether she liked the engraved heart or not. She was gone and he could never figure out what he had done wrong. He had gone over every day of their relationship recalling the very beginning when Johanna had turned sweet sixteen, and how he didn't have much money left from his pay checks from his job at the Hawthorne Melody Ice Cream Company where he worked after school stocking freezer shelves. He had to pay room and board to his parents. The money, unbeknownst to him, was deposited in a special saving account for him by his mother. Every penny he had left over was spent on Johanna. He even pilfered his piggy bank. Birthday money and Confirmation gifts that once found their way into the slot of the red and white porcelain pig were now lying on his bed in the attic. His love for her had to be expressed and buying presents was the only way he knew. He had pried open the cork in the white under belly, shaking out every coin. White Shoulders was the perfume she wore all the time. It drove him wild inside when she wore it. He bought her the biggest bottle he could afford. Surprised at how expensive something so small could be he opted for cologne because that was in a bigger bottle than the perfume. He didn't know the difference between the two. She had mentioned liking cashmere sweaters, and even though it was the middle of a heat wave, he bought her one; white and soft, his hand never feeling anything so luxurious. That was another lesson he had learned about the high cost of being in love. He also surprised her by taking her downtown to the Chicago Theater on a Saturday night.   That was followed by dinner at Henrici's where he couldn't understand half the items on the menu and finally settled for a Julienne salad. He then understood what a Julienne salad was and got the first of many questioning looks from Johanna about his decision making skills.

They had sat in the balcony, back row, necking, not caring what was on the screen. The theater was their dark, private sanctuary and it didn't make any difference to them if there were others seated around them glancing their way. To Stan, he and Johanna were the only two people in the palatial Chicago Theater on a Saturday night and falling deeper in love. A string of dates followed until they were together every day of the week and their parents began asking questions. Their answers were short, innocent, and giddy. They were two teenagers in love. They were going steady or, as either one would explain to whoever would listen, "We're engaged to be engaged."

Chapter 11

An entire life of tracing, questioning, blaming and fighting to forget had vanished. The wait was over. He wondered if time had been kind to her. At least she wasn't a grandmother he thought. She had told him that during the phone conversation they had after she had called to thank him for returning the ring. The next conversation wouldn't come until five years later. She was married, her second, to a high powered attorney specializing in new issues of corporate securities. It was his third marriage and his last, his heart so clogged with the good life that dynamite couldn't have opened his arteries. She had initiated the next call, *El B*, the widow. She related her own ups and downs and the challenges of trying to get her daughter to enter adulthood and keep her there.

"God, Stan," she had said, almost pleading, "she's pushing thirty and acting like a three-year-old." He listened about the adult child who had gone through three husbands in about as many years and now was a graduate student studying abnormal psychology and living with one of her professors.

There were other calls and then his nervous invitation for Thanksgiving that gave him the runs for two days. He wondered if he would be forced by Chicago's finest to make yet another trip around the O'Hare loop. Her plane had landed, according to his watch and her arrival information, thirty minutes ago. Travelers kept spilling out of the doors, dispersing, disappearing into cabs and buses, other passenger cars. His eyes kept tracing the series of glass doors wondering which one she would emerge from. More passengers flooded out, some with assorted styles and sizes of luggage in both hands, some looking lost as they lugged everything from designer suitcases to torn cardboard boxes held together with twine. Some cleared the exit doors in a near jog. Stan's mind wasn't jogging. It was setting the world's record for last second doubts. "Oh, man," he warned himself, questioning, "What have you done?" Then the questions sprinted through his mind. Had time and gravity brought havoc to that pretty face? What about those laughing eyes? Were they lined with crows' feet or eagle talons? And that body? Did it hang and sag? "Oh, God," he pleaded, "please don't be a smoker." He wondered if she was a junkie hooked on artificial tranquility and serenity courtesy of the pharmaceutical industry. Did white powder ever go up that very pert nose? "Please, oh, please," he begged, hearing himself, "don't be a credit card junkie." His statement was followed by a question challenging his rationality. "Credit card junkie?" he asked aloud. "Are you serious?" He shook his head. "Where is your head at? God, she was right about you, Stanley. Grow the fuck up." Then he felt a little better knowing her daughter and the professor would be spending Thanksgiving somewhere in New England.

The passengers kept coming and so did his doubts. "God, look at me," he said quietly. "She's going to hate me." He was mad at himself for not dressing up, for not wearing a tie. Dee had always insisted that he wear a tie, even if they went to the supermarket. "I'm dressed like a darned Geritol preppie," he blurted out. Suddenly, his repressed, seldom heard brash side jumped in. "Hey, if she doesn't like you the way you are, she can get on the next plane back to Boston. Corduroy sport jackets, Levis, Oxford cloth shirts with button down collars, white socks, and penny loafers are cool." Then his seldom heard angry self stuck in its two cents. He squinted, doubting, like his middle name, Thomas and said: "Ah, she can kiss my ass if she doesn't like the way I look."

Another swarm of passengers appeared and vanished. "Darn," he said, then seeing the Chicago police car stopping several cars behind him, the officer firmly urging the drivers to move on. "I'm not moving," he muttered, as the exiting passengers kept coming. He saw a lady, looking like what his cousin had called Miss Goodyear and lugging what appeared to be everything she owned. She came slowly through the door, other passengers squeezing by her. The lady stopped, catching her breath and her bearings and that's when he saw *El B* emerge around her. There was no doubt; still Sweet sixteen and direct from the pedestal. Not a trace of gravity. Their eyes met. He was at her front door, meeting her for the first time, a blind date set up by a friend of his. It was a date that was supposed to be a cruel joke. Johanna Pearson was known as Miss Ice Cube of Riverside-Brookfield High School and his friend and his friend's girlfriend thought it would be great fun to arrange a blind date. His friend's girlfriend disliked Johanna Pearson; more like envied her because of her beauty. Besides, what no one knew, not even his friend that his friend's girlfriend had missed her period. What his friend and his friend's girlfriend didn't miss was the sight of the two heads in the front seat disappearing from view once the film came on the screen at the drive-in movie.

* * * * *

Stan nonchalantly waved to Johanna as if the last time they had seen each other had been the day before. His eyes absorbed her and he nodded at the cop who was moving towards him, Stan's look telling him he was going to help the most beautiful girl in the world with her luggage. The cop nodded back and Stan tried desperately not to run to her. By the time she had finished waving back at him, her smile recognizing, he had skipped across two cab and limo lanes. He stopped, trying not to grin, and asked, "What took you so long? You helping the flight attendants clean up the cabin?" Out of habit he flicked the tip of her nose with the second knuckle of his curved index finger. They looked at each other not speaking.

Then she laughed and asked, "Where can a lady find a gentleman around here to help her with her luggage?"

"You found him," he said, relieving her of the garment bag she was carrying and taking the handle of the suitcase she was pulling, a smaller make-up case riding on top. "I moonlight here so I can afford to keep my women in White Shoulders."

She knowingly shook her head ever so slowly. "I knew you'd find your calling in life."

"Come on," he said, checking for a break in the traffic. "The constable has been looking for an excuse to tow my car ever since he saw me waiting for you."

Stan led interference for her through the traffic, surprising everyone, including a limo driver, by yelling at him after he had honked and almost hit them. "You ain't drivin' a cab in Tokyo, asshole," a hyper Stan shouted. He didn't see *El B's* smile. They were behind his car, the trunk popping open, when he carefully set the suitcase, garment bag and make-up case inside.

"Sorry about the potty mouth." His arms opened and he barely hugged her. "Welcome, to Chicago, Miss Johanna," he said. "Or, should I say, welcome back? Did you have a good flight?"

She hugged him back. "Any time the plane lands it's a good flight."

He looked at her, seeing the lines now, but remembering only White Shoulders, cashmere sweaters, and the drive-in movie. "Good to see you."

"And what's this surprise you told me about on the phone?"

He laughed enjoying having the upper hand. "If I told you, it wouldn't be a surprise."

* * * * *

The weekend was over. She had stayed two extra days. It had been at his request making Thanksgiving almost perfect. "You can avoid the holiday crunch back to Cambridge," he had said. "Neither of us needs the mob scene at the airport, and besides, you need time to enjoy my surprises.

The first surprise shocked *El B*. Stan had located her sister, Gale, and flew her in from Los Angeles. She showed up about the time they were going to sit down to the Thanksgiving dinner Stan had prepared. Joanna and Gale hadn't seen each other in almost thirty years. His cousin, the cop, had come through again. The sisters embraced and cried, teased and laughed, and gotten into several arguments. They parted at the airport Sunday afternoon, embracing, crying, teasing and laughing again, vowing to stay in touch, Gale ordering: "Next Thanksgiving is in LA, all of us, the family. Okay?" Then she disappeared into the terminal and the police waved his car on.

"I've got another surprise for you," he said nervously, as he inched his car through the heavy traffic of the Kennedy then exiting north at Cumberland leaving the packed expressway of creeping metal snails.

"First Gale and . . ."

"Be patient. I'll give it to you tomorrow on the way back to the airport." He suddenly felt a wave of depression. He glanced at her briefly. "It went by too fast, Johanna."

"I know."

They didn't say much, both feeling more emotionally than physically exhausted from the holidays together. They enjoyed Gale's visit and survived the call from Johanna's daughter on Thanksgiving morning. She was hysterical, having done battle with both the professor and his mother who she had met for the first time. She hated her even before their hands had come together in a brief, frigid shake. She had pleaded with her mother to fly to Chicago. Stan had defused that bomb with sincere tact and a promise of a later visit. Johanna had survived his three daughters, a son-in-law, boyfriend, and first date. The youngest, Dotty, the once teen-age rebel turned yuppie C.P.A., wasn't too thrilled that her father's old girlfriend would be sleeping at the house of her late mother and not at a hotel. Johanna defused that bomb with her own sincere tact during Thanksgiving dinner saying, "Your father and I are old friends and he's been a perfect gentleman and host."

"Yeah, darn it," he said, as Thanksgiving became thankful.

They did end the long weekend with his being a perfect gentleman even though he wanted to make love to her in the worst way. They had continued to visit the past where they explained and apologized, apologized and explained. Then they sheepishly took a peek into their futures, Stan admitting, "God, I'm scared to death of spending the rest of my life alone."

"You mean I'm not the only one?"

"I guess not." His hand rested on hers. "Have you ever been lonely?"

She nodded. "Try my second marriage."

"Really?"

"Really," she said. "Being with someone and feeling you're still by yourself is the worst feeling a person can have."

He barely stroked her hand. "I'll match your worst and raise you with loving someone with your entire being and not having her with you to share that love."

Her other hand rested on top of his. "I think it's time we let the past go, don't you."

"Consider it gone." Their hands gripped tightly together for a moment. "Could I interest the lovely lady in a glass of the bubbly?"

She jokingly removed her hands from his. "Sir, are you trying to ply me with liquor?"

"You bet."

"Then for heaven's sake what are you waiting for?"

He uncorked a bottle of champagne, they clinked glasses, took a sip, set the glasses down on the living room coffee table and it was the drive-in movie all over again including popcorn, gasping for air and moans that caused house lights to go on all over the neighborhood. They cuddled together on the living room sofa when he informed her, "My daughters said that people our age should be in bed by midnight."

"Your daughters said what?"

"Alone," he quickly added, and then started laughing. "You in your room and me in mine," he said, biting his cheeks.

They kissed goodnight and he escorted her to her room

where he hugged her and said, "I think I can handle another Thanksgiving like this."

"Even with all of the family drama I brought in that additional suitcase?

"Especially with the family drama," he said. "Plus, it'll be our turn to dump on the children."

"I kind of like the way your mind works."

The next morning he told her they would have to leave an hour earlier for the airport. "You saw that traffic yesterday when we dropped off your sister," he had said to her when she had questioned him. Then she said, "I thought the reason I was staying an extra day was so that we wouldn't have to fight traffic."

He was trapped and it was written all over his face. "Okay," he said. "You got me."

Her look said it all.

"It's a surprise," he said, trying to do damage control.

She looked at him not believing. "This surprise isn't the bum's rush, is it?" she asked without a smile, her eyes not sparkling.

"After all these years I'm going to throw you out?" He smiled and said, his words going over her head. "Get real."

He felt empty putting her luggage into the trunk of car that morning. There were no quarrels inside of him, no one lecturing him that this was for the best; that she was leaving; telling him pearls of philosophy like his father did in the boat somewhere on Lake of the Woods; like his grandfather, his empathy showing through his crusty exterior when he placed his hand on his grandson's shoulder and said, "The one that got away sometimes remembers they shouldn't have." His father was a vague image, but his mother was crystal clear, trying to be funny which she seldom was, doing a poor impersonation of Doris Day, jokingly singing off key, "K-Sorry; K-Sorry." That had been her pearl of philosophy to him when he had informed the family the day he had joined the Air Force.

* * * * *

He and Johanna rode west along Dempster without speaking. She didn't notice the first turn off the main street, but did when he turned into the parking lot. "This doesn't look like O'Hare field to me," she said, looking across the large field surrounded by trees.

"It's on the way," he said nervously, feeling like the forest preserve picnic grove had become a second home to him. He stopped the car, went around to the other side and opened the door like he had always done; like she expected. He took her hand and she squeezed back not letting up on her grip. They walked across the clearing sometimes kicking at the few stray leaves in their path that remained, their breath visible.

"Where are you taking me?" she asked innocently. "Into the woods for a nature stroll or do you have something more devious planned?"

"Kind of," he said, seeing the bare maple tree again, leading her to it. "Your surprise," he said nodding at the tree.

She didn't get it at first, shaking her head, questioning. "Am I missing something?" Then, following the direction of his index finger, she saw it.

"It's still there," he said, putting his arm around her waist, this time hers joining his. "The B's still here after all of these years."

She looked at him, tears unchecked, and said, "For eternity."

Her arms slipped around his neck. "I...."

He put his index finger on her lips. "Don't say a word," he said tenderly, a knuckled index finger brushing against her nose like a feather.

* * * * *

They stood embracing outside his car at the departure curb until a Chicago cop, unsmiling and appearing all business like, said in an uncharacteristically understanding voice, "It's time, folks."

He looked at her feeling like he did on their first date, "It's next Thanksgiving at Gales, right?"

"Right," she said, a slight curl to her lips. She took the handle of her suitcase, checked to see if the make-up case was secure, re-gripped her garment bag and started to walk towards the entrance way. Suddenly, she stopped and turned. "How 'bout next week in Cambridge?" she said, her invitation almost a command.

He winked. "I'll call you tonight."

"You'd better."

He flashed her thumbs up, shouting after her, "That's an order I'll follow any old time." His thumb was still extended up as he watched her head for the terminal door. In a moment she disappeared. He turned and saw a police car pull up along side of his car. He waved his hand as he jogged in between his car and the police. Nodding politely at the cop, he got into his car taking one last look at the entrance where she had entered. "Well, Stanley," he said smiling. "Looks like next week at this time you're surprise trip to the forest preserve is going to be converted into a ride on the MTA." He paused, pulling out into traffic, and then asked, "Will you ever return?"

PART III

I've Got a Secret

Chapter 1

Could anyone idolize a dictatorial immigrant Italian grandmother who drank Jim Beam from a Mason jar? Georgie could.

Georgie worshipped his gruff, despot grandmother, Nana Beam as she was lovingly known by him, because she did something no one else in his family or life did. She listened to him.

Nana Beam, AKA Dolores Deedee Filippini, did more than listen. She nodded at Georgie, who she called, Giorgio while he talked to her. Her kind brown eyes flashed love and understanding while she absorbed his every word. She said very little. Her words to Georgie, unlike those to other family members, were few and poignant; pearls of wisdom, each coated with a luster gathered over her seventy plus years. Those individual gems, lubricated with Jim Beam from her ever present Mason jar, helped nudge her grandson through the turmoil of a confused adolescence. Her listening made it easier for him from being forced to attend wakes with his family. His father the enforcer.

Nana Beam's few select words were also responsible for lovingly guiding her grandson through a chaotic early adulthood that included a divorce. She passed away before learning of a surprise received by her grandson. It was the biggest secret of all time and he didn't know if he would've had the courage to share it with her. The surprise secret shook

Georgie to his soul and might have well contributed to Nana Beam's demise instead of the Blessed Mother taking her as she often predicted.

* * * * *

Georgie read the obituary page every morning after attaining adult status. It was a habit he inherited from both his Nana Beam and his father, George, who referred to the daily listings of those who were, but now no more, as the Irish Scratch Sheet. Georgie's grandmother and father had identical thoughts when they read the obituary page. Both wanted to see the other's name in print looking back at them.

Georgie never forgot the reactions of his grandmother and his father coming from behind the newspaper. There were his father's glib, but reverend quips about the daily deceased, his attempts at humor, which he was all but void, with statements like: "If you don't see your name in print, you're going to have a good day." His father's face stayed buried behind the Chicago Tribune, the voice so monotone it put itself to sleep. "Waking up on the green side of the grass, even if you have a smashin' hangover, is better than being under the bloody sod," he had heard his father say many times in his adopted Irish brogue; Georgie's father was born in America and so were his parents. His father's grandparents, however, came from the Old Sod, refugees from the Potato Famine.

Nana Beam's comments about the same deceased were terse and to the point. When a name was recognized Georgie's grandmother would utter in her Italian accent, "You go wita God anda rest in peace." Her other limited comment was joined by a hand movement that sometimes included fingers and the touching of her face or arms. Her gesture meant she had put a curse on the deceased. The curse was preceded by one of two words indicating the gender of the deceased. "Cagna," she would hiss at a female. "Bastardo," was something Georgie understood at a young age having acquired an extensive vocabulary from listening to his Nana Beam vent. Georgie was also well versed in English profanity and colloquialisms having heard his father's verbal explosions; almost all were directed at him.

The only other evidence of life Georgie could see coming from his father and grandmother when either held the Tribune was the quiver coming from age spotted hands. The more the newspaper seemed to flutter in his father's hands on a particular morning, the more thankful his father was for being on the green side of the grass after saluting his dear old Ireland too many times the night before.

Nana Beam's quivering hands were caused by a combination of old age and old rage. The old rage was ongoing and directed at whoever got in her gun sights. It could be Georgie's father, mother or both, but her biggest salvos were unleashed during her weekly battle with her sister, Kate. Katarina or Kate was another name she prayed to see heading the Irish Scratch Sheet.

Georgie's father's hallmark of life was based on the family name; respecting one's heritage with a blind passion (only the Irish inherited the earth). Georgie knew all about respecting the family name and how actions often times were louder than words. He had seen his father display his hands like some form of unique tools. The palms were up, the thick, gnarled fingers looking like miniature, crooked tree branches displayed with pride. Georgie knew the words that accompanied the display.

"It's the sweat of your brow, Lad, that people notice. That and these here calloused mitts," his father would boast. "These hands ain't never seen any of those girlie aloe lotions, and that I can swear on me grandmother's grave."

According to Georgie's father, hard work consisted of two parts. The first part, lip synched by Georgie when he knew his father couldn't see him, consisted of, "You bust your ass to provide for your family." His father had done that. There was his job with Chicago's Bureau of Streets and Sanitation that drenched his t-shirts with sweat in the summer. His ears, fingers, toes numbed from frostbite in the winter along with a nose that turned blue. Those were his combat ribbons that he wore with pride. He displayed a chronic lower back ache like his collection of cheap bowling trophies lined up across the mantle in the living room that topped off the fake fireplace. He constantly made reference to toiling for his family's daily bread with a series of grimaces and assorted statements to his wife and son. He ignored his mother-in-law whenever he could. His spotlight focused on, "I broke my achin' G.I. back for you and this is the thanks I get." His father had never served in the military, flat feet and a punctured right ear drum kept him from marching off to Over There. Other parts of his father's anatomy, front or back, top or bottom, public or private could be substituted into the basic statement. Respecting the family name was the glue that tied hard work and providing for one's family together in a tight fist. There were also never ending sermons coming from his position of patriarchal prominence at the head of the antique oak table that barely fit in the kitchen. The sermons began with, "You work hard." That short growl of an introduction was generally followed by, "Don't do stupid things that give the morons of the world ammunition they can use to take pot shots at the family name." Stupid things were never specifically mentioned. Neither was his definition of morons. It was assumed that the consumption of too much wine, women and song were the major contributing causes for stupid things being done. That trio of things was talked about exclusively at Willie Maloney's Saloon two blocks from the house, his father's second home. Somehow, gossip, rumors and lies weren't included in his father's list that fueled his sermons; his particular preaching always coming to an end the same way with a threat: "If anyone in this family ever brings disrespect to our grand and glorious good name, I'll break every bone in his goddamned body."

Since Georgie was the only male child in the family, he knew exactly who was being targeted for candidacy into the Osteopathic Hall of Fame. His mother had been exempt long ago, having achieved sainthood. His father knew better than to ever point a finger at his wife, a blue ribbon award winning cast iron skillet swinger. Georgie's father also knew to stay clear of his mother-in-law. Nana Beam's use of another kitchen gadget—a solid wooden rolling pin--also had her being the recipient of another form of award, a blue ribbon attached to the seal of her divorce by the presiding judge, he of Italian heritage. "Dio ti benedica, signora," he had said to her as the gavel slammed down; a glare directed at her now ex-husband, his left arm being supported by a sling.

According to Georgie's father, the ultimate expressing of respect was summed up by actions. Those spoke louder than words and those actions were categorized and ranked according to his father's convoluted philosophy of life; that based on death, more precisely, the attending of wakes. "If you knew 'em, or knew of 'em," his father would start out, his monotone dripping with his most oft used statement, "you go and pay your respects to their family." For drama and emphasis, his father would lower the Tribune to a position just below his eyes. If he could have, his father would have added eight bars of organ music from St. Stanislaus Bishop and Martyr Church to his homily on respect. His father's stern brown eyes could melt glass or at least make it shatter. Georgie had learned to protect himself from breaking and melting by avoiding the twin laser beams and concentrating on what was on his plate. After two bites, his father's sinister look would disappear behind the paper.

Georgie hated going to wakes. His Nana made them palatable by whispering in his ear her special magical words. "Remember, afta, you father, he always go toa Maloney's Saloon." She would pull away from his ear, give him a smile and add, "Dat's where you geta da soda pop."

The older Georgie got the more surprised he became noticing an increase in the number of familiar names appearing in the Irish Scratch Sheet. His dislike of wakes ranked second behind his being called Georgie, a nickname his father had tagged on him during a rare sober moment. His father had no use for juniors or any name with a Roman numeral after it. "Pretentious crap," he would mutter. He was George Patrick Porter and his son was Georgie, George Michael by birth, made official by the sprinkling of Holy Water over his head at St. John Cantius Church just before the family moved north and west, away from what his father had logically reasoned, "Too goddamned many Wops moving in." The first move, one of two in Georgie's life, took place when he was an infant and the

Holy Water had barely dried on his fuzz covered head. The rationale for moving one's family, according to Georgie's father, was based on a particular group of inferior human beings contaminating his family. The particular group of inferiors changed whenever his father felt threatened; something he would never admit to. To inoculate and safeguard his family from disease, Georgie's father called on the Saints. "I got us a house in Saint Stanislaus Bishop and Martyr Parish," he had announced to his family. "We're movin'."

Saint Stanislaus Bishop and Martyr stayed a part of the Porter family even after the family had made its second move, this one, like the first, to the north and slightly west before Georgie started kindergarten. His father's rationale: "Goddamned Polacks are moving in and surrounding me like a pack of Blood Hounds."

Georgie could never understand his father's disdain for those of Italian or Polish heritage since Georgie's mother was of Italian and Polish ancestry and his grandmother, who lived with them, was one hundred percent Italian, coming to America along with her younger sister from the north of Italy.

Nana Beam had been part of an arranged marriage to a man who was believed to be Italian and an acquaintance of a distant relative in the Venice area. The man's name was Walo. Georgie's grand-mother fell in love with who she thought was a man of Italian decent. By the time she realized that Walo stood for Walowicz and he had a first name, Tomasz, she didn't care. She would emerge from her love struck trance later.

The main reason Saint Stan's Church stayed a part of the Porter family was Nana Beam. St. Stanislaus Bishop and Martyr was Nana Beam's favorite place in spite of an overwhelming

Polish congregation that drove her son-in-law into his move-the-family mode. Nana Beam didn't care where she lived as long as she could get to St. Stan's on the weekends. She didn't care that she didn't drive. Her son-in-law did. He was her chauffer. She didn't drive because of double vision in one eye caused by Walo slapping her one evening at dinner when she served him ravioli instead of pierogi.

St. Stanislaus Bishop and Martyr church had what every grandmother dreamed of. There were confessions on Saturday afternoon; weekend evenings featuring card and Bunco games in the church's basement social hall and Bingo on Sunday afternoon after Mass. Weekends were the only time when Nana Beam smiled.

If it hadn't been for Georgie's grandmother living with her daughter and son-in-law in an add-on room attached to the back of their brick bungalow, Georgie would have experienced martyrdom before reaching the midway point of puberty. His father had his whipping boy and, although never at the receiving end of the leather lash, his father's words tore into Georgie's flesh and soul until fear, not love, was what he had for his father.

Nana Beam, as she was respectfully addressed by one and all except her sister, treated the Irish Scratch Sheet as her social calendar. She knew twice the number of deceased than her son-in-law did, and she attended all the wakes dragging her family with her. When a wake was on the docket a family reunion would ensue. Nana Beam made sure of it. The extended Porter family included a half dozen or so relatives, the male relatives, like Georgie, attending under duress. Nana's family included only her younger sister, Katarina who she did verbal battle with the moment introductory pleasantries had been completed and condolences passed on to the deceased's survivors.

Nana Beam's sister had two married daughters, Monica and Maria, each with two children, a boy and a girl. Nana was called Deedee by her sister and she was the only one in the family who would dare use that name. Katie and Deedee appeared to hate each other. Phones got slammed down, dinners ended with a turned over chair or two and slamming doors that rattled the windows cut visits short. The rattling was punctuated with curses placed on one or the other sister in Italian. Those curses came complete with the obligatory hand and finger gestures along with the closing of either eye or the raising of an eye brow. Sometimes, if the argument was extremely heated, hands, fingers, eyes and brows merged into twin miniature mushroom clouds.

Georgie's mother, Anna was restricted to addressing Nana as Mama at home or introducing her as Madre outside her residence. She dreaded her mother and Katie meeting, and that included Christmas Day, at any Mass, even the Feast Day of St. Catherine of Sienna. Anna would step into her customary role as peacemaker only to end up being pummeled by her mother's broken English and temper tantrums.

Both Georges tried to distance themselves from the sisters at wakes and numerous family functions, usually Sunday afternoon pasta dinners. Georgie loved those dinners even though his Nanas Beam and her sister spent most of the time arguing in the kitchen. Heated exchanges exploded over a steaming kitchen range and included such world shattering matters as, "Mama pinched her ravioli shut with her fingers not a fancy fork."

George Porter liked Katie's husband, Sean a jovial, crimson cheeked Irishman who could sing every Irish folksong ever written, especially after starting his second six pack of Harp. Besides, Sean accompanied himself on the ukulele which he learned from one of his football teammates when he played for Michigan State in the early 1950's; his teacher a Hawaiian place kicker from Honolulu who could kick a football from East Lansing into Lake Michigan. Somehow, home or away, Sean's Uke made an appearance, especially if beer was present.

Georgie made friends with the husbands of Katie's daughters even though they were older. Tony Ricci was married to Gloria a pretty dark haired girl with huge alluring brown eyes. He was a part-time bookmaker and aspiring pop music vocalist. His imitation of Frank Sinatra earned three and a half stars out of five. Georgie's father referred to Tony as, "That Goddamned no talent Grease Ball who has a voice like a wet fart." In public, pleasantries and complements described Tony Ricci.

Katie's other daughter, Maria, was living with a part-time actor and full-time waiter. Duke Mongan desperately wanted to reverse the waiter and actor roles but made a good living in a high end restaurant in downtown Chicago. Georgie enjoyed Duke's stories of his experiences of meeting celebrities at auditions for acting jobs that he never got.

Nana Beam stayed cordial with her sister's daughters. Once they left and the fallout from the mushroom clouds had dissipated, Nana Beam returned to being, according to her son-in-law, a dictatorial shrew who had been run out of Italy. "That woman probably had Mussolini begging to be hung up by his heels," he had often said to Georgie's mother because he hated

Nana Beam dictating every breath inhaled and exhaled in the Porter household.   Georgie's father took his mother-in-law's strong willed behavior in stride.   Over the years he thanked God for providing bountiful harvests of the grain and the grape for helping to maintain his sanity.

Georgie never had a problem with his Italian name.   He loved to hear it in Nana Beam's broken English and it helped him eradicate his father's pet name for him and bury the rationale behind it.

"Hey," he heard his father say way too often, his mouth hidden by the Tribune.   "You're named after two saints, one a dragon slayer and the other, a battle tested angel who could kick the crap out of both Satan's and Mussolini's armies."   His father's head would disappear behind the paper followed by a statement and a question.   The statement: "Even the Greeks could kick the crap out of Mussolini's army.   His ending comment was always: "Faith and be Jesus, Amen."

Georgie didn't put much credence into his father's rationale for names.   He did, however, believe as Gospel every word that his Nana Beam ever uttered to him.   Her litany of saints from the north of Italy where her family roots were entrenched put blessing upon blessing on her grandson and gradually, with the help of countless decades of the rosary, had him replacing Georgie with Giorgio and later George.   The final change over in names took place just before his father had been mentioned in the Irish Scratch Sheet.   Two short weeks after his father died Nana Beam's name appeared on the Tribune's Obituary page.   Prior to making that cherished list, she managed to put a host of curses on her sister and spit on her son-in-law's grave at Our Lady of Mt. Carmel cemetery.   Georgie's grandmother loved spitting on images that she didn't like, her spit accompanied by a select creative curse.

Georgie had cried when he said his final goodbye to his grandmother. He loved Nana Beam. She always listened. When his life was in crisis, his marriage ending, she listened and nodded, muttering her single favorite word describing her grandson's soon-to-be-ex-wife: "Puttana." Nana was his idol. Often he thought about the altar on which he had placed her and shook his head. "How could you possibly idolize an old lady who drank straight bourbon from a jar, placed curses on people and spit on the others she disliked?" he had asked himself countless times. A knowing smile would creep across his somber face, his head going slowly from side to side while his heart and soul felt the glow of her memory. She had helped him as a troubled youngster, as a troubled teen and a troubled young adult get through the difficult times in his life. She was there for him watching as his vow of Holy Matrimony disintegrated. She was there for him after his divorce when he lived in a dank basement studio apartment complete with every mouse in the City of Chicago as room-mates. She was there for him as the wise grandmother; a bourbon filled Mason jar in her hand, knowing about her Giorgio's true love and his illicit romance with Maggie Stephenson.

"Sounds likea nice a girl, Giorgio," she said, her head going slowly from side to side. "Buta she's a not for you." The knuckles of her index fingers rubbed at her sad moist eyes. "You married, Giorgio. The Commandments forbid," she continued, her head still going from side to side. "God and a Holy Catholic Church forbida," she said her eyes suddenly dry and serious. "Say, arrivederci to her."

Georgie knew she was right. He also knew that he had violated the Number One Porter Commandment. His divorce brought shame on his family. Reasons didn't matter. Commandments were commandments; especially those set down by his father, and had to be obeyed. Even Nana Beam knew that the Commandments ruled. She still stood on a pedestal atop her grandson's altar; an idol who could do no wrong.

Chapter 2

Even before Georgie got engaged his father had questioned his son's sanity about his choice of females. His son's sane state of mind was always discussed at Maloney's Saloon; never at home even though Georgie's mother and Nana Beam harbored similar concerns.

"You must have rocks in your head, Lad," his father had said to Georgie after first meeting Patrice Ryan. "She's Irish by name only," he continued. "Those hands of hers have never seen a kitchen sink full of dirty dishes and soapy water." His head went barely budged from side to side. "I'm willing to bet she's never peeled a potato in her life."

Georgie thought it was just his father being his usual negative, sarcastic self. What surprised him was that his Nana Beam wasn't much more diplomatic even though she expressed her feelings on a somewhat limited basis. There would be a slow, side-to-side shaking of her head, slightly faster than his father's and a forlorn look cemented on her lined face before she uttered, "Notta for you, Giorgio."

Georgie knew that Nana Beam prayed for him. Her prayers were more like warnings to the Blessed Mother. "You no letta my Giorgio marry that *puttana* if you know what's a good for you," she would whisper reverently, her fingers almost pulverizing each scarred bead of her worn rosary. She knew better than to put a curse on the Blessed Mother and settled for her version of a subtle reminder at the end of her prayers instead of using, Amen. Nana Beam, like her son-in-law, viewed Georgie's future wife as immoral.

Georgie didn't see Patrice in the same way as his family and friends did. All he could see were alluring, hypnotic hazel eyes, a pair of curvaceous legs that started at State and Madison and ended at the Illinois State Line plus the nicest boobs he had ever laid eyes on.

Nana Beam always found time to listen to her Giorgio. She never interfered with his life, only offering a plethora of orders camouflaged as suggestions. A particular suggestion always started out, for example, by Nana Beam saying, "Giorgio, does dis lady frienda yours ever puta on a nice a dress? Like something she coulda wear to Mass?"

Georgie would always smile and be polite to his grandmother and reply to her concern. "Patrice is very fashion conscious, Grandma," he would say, defending the woman he was going to marry. "She's with the times, Nana. You know, modern." He didn't tell her that his fiancé was an agnostic and threw a fit when she found out she would have to be married in church or not at all. As Georgie would learn, the auburn haired beauty didn't take lightly to ultimatums. She didn't take to marriage or motherhood either even though she gave birth to two exquisitely beautiful children; a boy and a girl. The children would later be used as pawns in a divorce, and put Georgie on giant guilt-trips that led him to the threshold of the poorhouse.

After her prayers and during her talks with her Giorgio, Nana Beam carried on her tradition of taking a sip from her jar and then slipping her grandson a five spot for spending money. Her son-in-law often remarked to his wife, "Your mother has never given us a dime while she's lived here. I bet that cheap old broad still has her First Communion money."

In between her words of wisdom to her grandson, her spiritual warnings and generosity, Nana Beam would savor her Jim Beam, her jar never being empty. Georgie first started listening to his grandmother as a small boy as he plodded through the years of growing up. He endured everything from being called Georgie Porgy to Georgie Girl and whatever other cruel form of creativity one prepubescent human being could concoct to humiliate another prepubescent human being. Nana Beam and her Mason jar were there to console Georgie. Several times in the early years her words of consolation included instructions on the manly art of self defense when several bullies entered the picture. "You kicka dem as hard as you can right dare," she ordered, her bourbon container pointing at her Giorgio's crotch. "Den you planta you shoe uppa dare culo. You have no more problems."

Nana Beam quickly became Georgie's hero as well as his idol.

Georgie's grandmother had discovered long ago that bourbon killed pain better than homemade Italian red wine. Using the name Dago red to describe the wine of her Italian heritage infuriated her. During a broken marriage that came complete with broken bones, Georgie's grandmother taught her husband a lesson he never forgot. A scar has a way of acting as a reminder. Before the second bone was being threatened, she took a rolling pin to the head of Walo. Several other swings bounced off his right ear creating a permanent hum, barely missed breaking his jaw and careened off his shoulders and arms as he tried desperately to save his life. He didn't have enough hands and arms to keep her from breaking his nose, the rolling pin gouging out a nasty chunk of flesh above the bridge making him look like a middle linebacker who had spent way too many seasons in the N.F.L. using his head as a battering ram. There were also scars left from her shouts. "I'm a gonna shove dis uppa you *culo*." A fractured skull and a dislocated shoulder sent Walo packing.

There wasn't much that got Nana Beam riled. The derogatory terms, Dago, Grease Ball and Wop brought out her ire, but no deadly weapon. If there was even a hint of her son-in-law disrespecting her daughter, Nana Beam would let him know. "Who do ya tink you married to?" she would shout at him. "A Sicilian?" Other agitators in her life centered on lack of attention paid to her by her Giorgio and his parents and the absence of good television programs in the evening where she commandeered the television remote in the Porter living room.

Chapter 3

Over the years, Georgie had knelt at the knees of his grandmother soaking up her pearls of philosophy and subtle guidelines. There was no kneeling before he married Patrice. He knew what Nana Beam would say and he was too much in love to take advice. Then, after his world had turned into what subtle guidelines couldn't cure, he knelt by her side, his sobbing face buried in her lap.

Nana Beam sat and stroked the back of her Giorgio's neck, listening and saying nothing. What she was thinking would've shocked her Giorgio, his mother and father and brought accolades from her sister, Katie. A rolling pin made up the crux of her thoughts.

Georgie found bravery that he never knew he had when he told his grandmother that he had sinned. Not only had he sinned, but he broke one of the Ten Commandments.

His grandmother had listened, continued stroking his neck and even dried his tears. "You go to confession," she had softly said. "I pray to the Blessed Mother for you. You no worry. The Blessed Mother and I are likea dis," she continued, showing her grandson her middle and index fingers almost twisted in a braid.

Georgie believed, and his grandmother's prayers were answered. They weren't the answers that Georgie had hoped for, but they did bring him peace.

Then Nana Beam found another form of peace. She didn't

wake up one morning and her pearls of philosophy never left Georgie's heart and soul. He would always worship his grandmother. He would cherish those memories of her, the lessons generally coming with the subtle wag of her index finger joined by one of two words repeated several times. It was, "Never, never, never," or "Always, always, always."

Nana Beam's wake was one he both dreaded and cherished. He found himself not wanting to say goodbye and let her go. He was that way with his mother at her funeral, but he let her go. Sadness and relief was what he felt when the cover to his father's casket was closed. As he stood in the back of the funeral parlor watching mourners pay their respects to the late Dolores Deedee Filippini--she had dropped the Walowicz when she put her rolling pin back in the kitchen drawer--he realized how much wakes had been an important part of his life.

His mother had loved going to wakes. They were like a night out on the town. She renewed acquaintances and caught up on gossip. Newborns were discussed as pictures of the infants were passed around. Nana Beam was smack dab in the middle of it all paying each newborn her form of compliment, designating what side of the family the little one resembled and giving thanks to the Blessed Mother.

Georgie's father had a different take on those who attended wakes besides himself. "Those people are all a pain in the ass," he would say the next morning, the Irish Scratch Sheet doing a version of its shaking dance. Obviously, he didn't include himself in the pain-in-the-ass category. His father would always insist on stopping for a drink on the way home, in his words, "It's the fitting proper thing to do to honor the deceased." There was never a single, solitary drink for his father who came home after a wake almost in the same condition as the rigid remains he had said his customary Our Father, Hail Mary, and Glory Be to earlier.

When Georgie was a child he had looked forward to going to wakes with his parents and Nana Beam for one reason. It wasn't the wake itself. Those he couldn't stand, most times sitting as far away from the deceased as possible waiting for his parents and grandmother to finish their visiting. He knew his father would insist on stopping at Maloney's afterwards for a drink and that meant there would always be a bottle of soda pop handed to him, a commodity rarely seen in the Porter house. On nights when his father was in a good mood, there would also be a bag of potato chips or pretzels for Georgie. He would sit on the barstool next to his mother and sip his pop trying to make it last. Fear prevented him from asking for a second bottle. Fear was also the reason he sat next to his mother. He had been chastised one too many times by his father for swiveling back and forth on the barstool, once being lifted up by one arm and getting a swat across his butt. "Goddammit, Georgie, sit your little ass still." The admonishment minus the swat had been followed by one from his mother directed at his father. That didn't last long because his father cut her off by ordering another drink. There were no potato chips or pretzels that night.

Nana Beam couldn't stand her son-in-law's saloon tantrums. She refrained from grabbing the nearest hard object, usually one of Maloney's solid glass ashtrays, and smacking him across the skull. Making a scene was something she avoided except when her and her sister would declare war on each other. She would count to ten in Italian and then take Georgie by the hand, almost yanking his arm from the socket, and drag him out to his father's old De Soto and sit in the car even though the Porter house was less than two blocks away.

Years went by, Baptisms and the Last Rites continued and the Irish Scratch Sheet, along with his Nana Beam, continued to dictate his mother and father's social calendar. During those years, Georgie had grown to despise his dad's drinking. Once he learned to drive he was relieved that he could avoid the scary rides home where his mother would warn his father about drinking and driving and his father, in turn, saying to his mother in a slur, "I'm as slobber and a yudge." His father never said a word to his mother-in-law. He glared a lot. Nana beam out glared him, only because he had to keep his eyes on the road.   Georgie would eagerly volunteer to drive after discovering the two magic statements for his mother and grandmother's sanity and safety. "Dad, have one for the road," he would whisper in his father's ear. "I'll drive." From the very first time he mustered enough courage to mutter the magic statements, his father was totally agreeable. Most times, the one for the road, was several more. He and his mother would lug him to the car while his grandmother would follow behind laying out a string of curses on her son-in-law that sounded both vile and filthy. "You *melagrana*," she would hiss at her target with a significant hand gesture. "*Carciofo*," was spit out at his back. A series of hand and finger movements punctuated with real spit ended her displeasure. Her most severe gesture really wasn't. It just sounded that way because of all of the emphasis she put on the phonetic pronunciation. "You *fungo*," she said in almost a growl that sounded like a death threat. Fungo would be strung out until it sounded like she was saying,

"Phhhuuuuunnnng," the 'o' silent. Fungo got both eye brows and hands moving along with a glare. In reality, Nana Beam had called her son-in-law a pomegranate, artichoke and mushroom respectively.

Once in the passenger side front seat of the car, Georgie's father would fall asleep before Georgie had turned the key in the ignition, a smudge of hair oil decorating the passenger side window.

About the same time his driver's license came into his life, Georgie started trying to shake the *I* from between the *G* and the *E* at the end of his name. "It makes me sound like I'm two years old," he had said, his mother and grandmother on the receiving end of his frustration. The *G* and the *E* squeezed tighter, trying, but not quite choking the life from the *I* that, thanks to his father's alcohol laced insistence, stayed cemented in its designated position. "As long as you're livin' in my goddamned house, you're Georgie," his father had said. "And don't forget it."

Georgie didn't. The *I*, however, coughed and gasped before slowly disappearing. That took place before his father, Nana Beam and his mother died and Georgie had been married for almost two years. His *I* disappeared about the time fate came calling in the form of Maggie Stephenson. She entered his life and he walked into a wall.

He was married to Patrice, the father of one with a second on the way. Patrice couldn't understand why her husband kept on with school saying, "Why bother? You'll end up being just like your father and those idiot male relatives of yours." Georgie hated confrontations with his wife. He wasn't fearful of losing his temper or getting physical with her. That wasn't

Georgie. Applying one of his grandmother's curses on his wife was a big concern. He knew them all and had seen them work. "I'm going to school so I can get a better job and give you the kind of life style you want," he had said to her. "The life style you even demand," he added for good measure.

"I hope you plan on finding an oil well on Austin Avenue in front of Wright Junior College," she would say, her sarcasm greater than usual.

Georgie's dream was to work with abused children. Then he got the word that his father had been killed. His dad had wrapped himself and his prized antique De Soto around a lamp post a block from home. The car was a collector's dream and his father had kept it in meticulous condition, shunning several lucrative offers to sell it. After the accident, the only buyer was a junk yard. Georgie's mother and Nana Beam should have been passengers in the car, but, according to Nana Beam, "The Blessed Mother she was a looking down on a you mother and me." They had been returning from a wake and a side trip to Maloney's Saloon for a quick drink. One quick drink led to another quick drink and another. His father more than likely assumed that his son was swiveling merrily away on the bar stool next to his mother and that he would be driving him home. He forgot that his son was married and at home with his pregnant wife and year old child. Georgie's mother and grandmother survived the wreck by opting to walk the two blocks back to the house. If they hadn't, they would have ended up joining Georgie's father looking like the De Soto that had turned into an accordion stepped on by a herd of stampeding elephants. With her husband gone, Georgie's mother had decided to join him, allowing her heart and soul to slowly die off. Georgie had no idea. No one did; not even an intuitive Nana Beam.

Georgie finished at Wright Junior College. He felt a sense of accomplishment albeit brief and met with his wife's demeaning remarks. Undaunted, he continued to be the *Little Engine That Could* and enrolled at De Paul University. There were no fraternity beer parties and Blue Demon basketball games for him. He worked days to support his wife and family and never had any money for himself. Patrice, not thrilled with the lack of money and her husband's absence, became more sarcastic and turned their tiny apartment into a state of constant agitation in the process. About the only thing she said to her husband was, "I wasn't put on this earth to change diapers full of shit because you never heard of birth control."

Georgie tried to shake off the sarcasm. Soon he found himself dreading to step foot into his own apartment. The solution to his problem, of sorts, was to stay away even more. He tended bar on the side at Maloney's telling Patrice he had a library night once a week for his class at DePaul. She shunned him even more.

Working at Maloney's gave Georgie a breather and most of the money he made he gave to his mother. He also slipped a fiver to Nana Beam instead of the other way around. His mother's indifference to life kept increasing even though the appearance of her granddaughter momentarily lifted the dark grey curtain covering her eyes. After Georgie's father had died, Georgie's mother's didn't wait very long to join her. It was the last wake he ever attended until Maggie Stephenson reappeared in his life.

Chapter 4

Georgie still read the Irish Scratch Sheet like his father. The only difference was he was living alone in the family house. His father, Nana Beam and mother were gone as was his marriage. He had been alone and lonely but, there was no self-pity flowing through his veins. His father wouldn't have allowed it. Georgie knew exactly what his father would have said to him had he lived; his very last statement expressing Porter's Family Law: "You brought dishonor to the family name by leaving my two grandchildren." He fantasized that his father would have also added: "Can't say that I blame you for dumping that nose-in-the-air bitch you married 'cause you let your little head control the big head." Georgie knew that compassion would not have been part of his father's remarks.

As he perused the Irish Scratch Sheet each morning, he'd come across a familiar name, read the details of a life summed up in a terse paragraph and then ignore his father's edict of showing respect for the dead. Then, one morning years later, before the first bitter sip of his morning coffee barely got by his lips, he saw her name and he found his fingers digging through every pearl that both his father and Nana Beam ever passed on to him.

"I'll just slip in and slip out," he told himself, knowing that the Porter family name would have no bearing in this situation. His concern was he didn't want people to know who he was or the real reason why he was there. Rest in peace was for parents, relatives and friends, the flow of one's tears in proportion to the personal attachment. His mother had received a flood; Nana Beam a tidal wave, unknown faces, all appearing to look like they had ancestors in Italy, packed the funeral parlor. Half, if not more, of the parishioners from Stanislaus Bishop and Martyr, mostly her card and bingo playing buddies, offered him never ending condolences. It appeared that he wasn't the only one Nana Beam had slipped fivers to in times of need. As for his father's wake, nary a tear drop was spilled. There weren't that many eyes in attendance.

He didn't know how he would react when he saw her. The last time had been one he never forgot. It wasn't the sex, the one and only time they made love; his grievous sin that would have brought on his father's wrath had he known. He had told his Nana Beam and received her patented sympathetic look along with her unforgiving shaking head. His choked up, whispered words of, "Farewell, my love," had stayed tattooed in his soul. That's what he remembered. She had looked so beautiful, so angelic, her head barely causing an indent on the soft, down pillow of her bed. He had kissed her on the forehead, the sound of her sleep barely audible, then tip-toed from her room and made his way slowly along the left side of the apartment's narrow hallway so the wooden floor wouldn't creak. He turned the front door knob, hesitated, then stepped out. His eyes looked back into her apartment trying to see through the dark, see around corners and see into her bedroom. He had never felt emptier as he reluctantly eased the door shut and then heard the lock click. His new life, the exciting one that had been filled with glorious guilt coated love, had suddenly turned to one awash in anguish. He had no way of knowing, feeling the way he did that night staring blankly at the dark oak door with the ugly varnish drip marks, that anguish would become his new best friend. That had been almost thirty years ago and there was a part of his being that had remained empty without her every single day since the dull, dead clicking sound of the lock finalized that farewell.

Georgie struggled against the teeth chilling March wind watching for a break in the traffic, a combination walk/jog/sprint for his life across the four lanes of Skokie Road to the funeral home ready to kick in. As he waited for his chance, he cursed the funeral home for not having a big enough parking lot and pulled his coat collar up until the top of his head and his eyes were the only parts of him getting the brunt of the icy wind. The instant he had seen her name and picture blaring at him from the Tribune's obituary page, his soul exploded, memories of the past grabbing at him like a wild river overflowing its banks after a torrential spring downpour. He read every word that was printed about her, digested every punctuation mark and was surprised at how she looked in the accompanying picture, still an incredibly cute preppie after decades. Then he read and continued to digest the words and picture again like a gourmand. Unlike savoring the banquet before his eyes, he couldn't shake the anguish that was seeping from within him. The finality of her life brought down his curtain of repressed hope in a deafening crash. There was the headline in bold type across two columns, **Noted North Shore Educator**. He had no way of knowing how old the picture was. His memory saw the sleeping form of his relaxed princess, the result of their love making and way too many Brandy Stingers that last night when he picked her up in front of her apartment on Hinman. They had driven just across the Evanston city limits into Rogers Park to a lounge on Clark called the Intimate Wick for a drink and a friendly talk. It was to have been a realistic farewell, a one last *Hi* and *Bye* of the two words that had originally brought them together. This was to be a cordial parting of two passengers on different ships sailing in opposite directions towards different horizons. They had been together for the six weeks of summer school at DePaul; three nights a week, three hours a night for six weeks. Then Tuesday and Thursdays entered the picture. They had quickly rationalized those days as extra study sessions to work on a class group project. There was no group project and neither wanted summer school to end. They each found ways to see each other, he constructing creative lies. His excuses for the extra time away from a very pregnant Patrice were coated in academic necessity. "Darn it, Patrice," he would start out almost pleading. "I need the library time." He would hold his thumb and forefinger up showing a sliver of light. "I'm this close to finally graduating; to finally making a life for us, to at last be able to give you things you want in life, the things I've always wanted to give you." She blasted him with a daily litany blaming him for her woes because, in her dull razor blade slashes, "You're a wimp, a fuckin' loser and in the clutches of that mean old bitch of a grandmother of yours."

"It's for my degree," he had said to Patrice, who had shut him off and out. "I'm working with a group. It's our project. It's important. I just can't walk out on them." Then he added something that surprised him and gave him a great deal of pleasure, if only for a moment. "With them I'm not a wimp or a fuckin' loser. I'm learning how to help troubled kids. I'm not a graduate of the Patricia Stevens Modeling School walking around with my nose in the air like I think my shit's ice cream and everyone should have a double dip."

Patrice could have been a model. She had poise and grace besides knowing how to apply make-up and, even when pregnant, got looks filled with lust. She never got beyond the surge in her ego that accompanied the feeling of turning heads; savoring eyes that flashed envy.

Georgie and Maggie kept meeting once summer school ended. They met until the first snow flurries came off Lake Michigan. He was finally going to graduate. The academic oriented excuses had run out along with other excuses. Then they both knew it couldn't go on. They had made their pact; sealed it with a hand shake. Then the hand shake turned into a hug and the friendly talk turned into his whispering words of love to her while they slow danced in the near darkness of the cocktail lounge. Neither had to be reminded of what the juke box filled with old songs was telling them; one in particular about, *Breaking up is very hard to do*. Now she was gone and the break up was more than very hard to do and more than final. Forever was now definite.

As he stepped into the entrance of the funeral parlor he felt a shiver. Then it was gone as the door sealed out the harsh wind that had tried to force its way in, to follow on his coattails as if he deserved more of the cold hammering. His face reappeared from his coat collar and his shoulders did an icy shrug. Then, for some bizarre reason, he thought of a movie he had seen as a boy. There was a song in that movie about pin-up girls and windblown skirts.   As he stood in the foyer, his wool lined trench coat now draped over his arm, he kept hearing the words about the March wind blowing petticoats that had too much starch.   He found himself mouthing the words: ...*For when it blows it scratches.*

   She had been his pin-up girl, even posing for him once in the living room of her apartment.   It was on a hot sultry evening after class.   She giggled standing in awkward, amateurish poses in her bra and panties; her giggles accentuated by her two gin and lemonades on an empty stomach.   His own hands shook as he tried to hold his dad's old Polaroid camera steady, hoping the film wasn't out of date.   That was a far cry from the innocence of their first meeting in the De Paul University bookstore when he walked into the end of a shelf of psychology books because he couldn't take his eyes off of her.   He never saw the flirting.   He was just being nice, or thoughtful, or polite, or stupid, or whatever he felt the first time he saw her.   Then it was too late.   When he had the opportunity to do the right thing, to say the married word, he suddenly didn't feel married; didn't want to be married; at least not to Patrice.   Instead, he clammed up, embarrassed at finding himself in a position he didn't know how to handle, and too curious to care that cats ran out of lives.   He was fascinated and excited, his ego enjoying its inflated status and reminding himself, "George Porter, you ain't no loser."   There had been playful flirting at first, talking during the break in class, passing notes back and forth with jokes about the professor and William Shakespeare.   He was back in the eighth grade again savoring his secret crush on the petite peroxide blond, Millicent Krenz and loving every nervous minute.   Then the flirting had started to get out of hand with their hands getting into the flirting and he backed away. The look on his face told her he wasn't available, shouldn't be available, and couldn't be available. She had cried; her tears making him feel like he had no ego to inflate. He held her. Then, in the quiet of the third floor apartment she shared with three other girl friends that were away in Europe for the summer, they mutually agreed through a series of silent hugs that they would continue to see each other until school was over. After all, they had rationalized; they were sitting next to each other in class three nights a week.

Georgie saw the brass stand, white block letters stuck on black poster board announcing that she was in Parlor B. He had moved across the funeral parlor foyer and down the hallway without realizing it until he was staring at a large **B**. He saw a portion of the casket through the crowd waiting in line to pay their respects to Maggie Louise Stephenson. She had been Dr. Stephenson, teacher, principal, and assistant superintendent and survived by a son, George Michael, his name. The obituary didn't mention the cause of death.

"Why give a reason," he had said, after putting down the paper. "She's not coming back. Nobody listed in the Irish Scratch Sheet ever does."

The finality hadn't set in until now as he waited in line; his one sided conversation trying to convince him not to go any further. "What the hell's the matter with you, Giorgio?" he asked. "What are you trying to prove?" He had hoped for an answer from his Nana Beam, but none came. He shuffled along in the stop-and-go line still finding it hard to believe that the first time he saw her had been summed up in two one syllable words that hadn't been mentioned in the obituary, but jumped out of the article and caused the paper to tremble the way it used to in his father's hands. Those two simple, innocent words sandwiched his first glimpse of her, the short frosted hair, petite figure, and the Miss Preppie banner running diagonally across her chest. He smiled, nodded and muttered, "Hi." She had smiled, nodded and said, "Hi," hers much more distinctly and friendly than his. Then there was his friendly, almost comical, "Bye," a mumbled, stupefied babble as he watched her continue in the opposite direction. She also said, "Bye," hers more of a sing-song friendly version. Then she was out of his life, as he recalled, at six o'clock during that first of June evening, and he didn't want her gone. He had spun his head around, his tongue and brain unable to connect to add on to the Bye as he watched the back of her walk toward the book store's door. That's when he ran smack dab into the flat end of the book shelve. He found his face plastered up against the blue lettering of *DePaul University Book Store* looking at a card identifying psychology text books, titles ranging from *Adjustment and Personality* to *The Abnormal Personality,* to *The Psychology of Adjustment* to *The Psychology of the Christian Marriage* to *Catholics: Living and Loving in Marriage.* His eyes did a once over of the titles. He had bought and read them all for his classes then selling them so he could scrape together enough money for the books required in his next classes. As foolishness replaced the dumb look and he peeled his red face from the shelf panel, he quickly headed in the direction for his classroom. Becoming dumb and foolish had replaced the feelings of wimp and loser. He didn't care. This would be his last summer night class. One more semester remained. When the fall would roll around, it would be one down and no more to go. He would have his degree before

Christmas.

With the start of a new session his intent had been, like every night class he attended, to kill time before enduring almost three hours more of his quest for a bachelor's degree. He always laughed when he remembered one of his high school teachers saying, "The mind can only absorb what the seat can endure." He had left work that fateful day at five like always. He parked the dump truck he drove for the Chicago Park District's Division of Forestry, used the men's room in the garage to get out of his scuffed, worn work boots, jeans, and sweaty T-shirt. He washed up at the stained sink splashing water under his arms and everywhere else above his waist and got dressed for class. Rush hour traffic was light on the way into Lincoln Park, and surprisingly he even found a parking spot down the street from Kelly's Pub where he squeezed his beat up Chevy into a space better suited for a Volkswagen. He walked into Kelly's to watch the tail end of the Cubs game, eat a bag of greasy, salty Yo-Ho potato chips, his supper, and wash it down with a bottle of Schlitz. His entire life, it seemed, had been spent going to night school even though it had only been a handful of years since his dad died. It had been quite a come down from the start of his first year at De Paul after transferring from Wright when his dad entombed himself in the massive old De Soto. He didn't have a chance to celebrate or drown sorrows after a Blue Demon basketball game back then; maybe even put the moves on a coed. He wanted to, thought about it, but he was a married man and just getting adjusted to parenthood when a second announcement of another pregnancy rode along with him each evening to and from school. The baby wouldn't be due until late January and he would have long since graduated. Before Santa Claus arrived he hoped he could start living like a normal human being. Normal, it appeared, was something of a fantasy because, as he had discovered, former Patricia Stevens Modeling School graduates with attitudes and over inflated egos had different views of normal. He could hear Nana Beam calling him a pomegranate and mushroom in Italian. He could feel her hand stroking the back of his head while she softly chastised him in her unique way asking, "Giorgio, why you breaka da Commandment?"

Chapter 5

He felt incredibly stupid after his not-so-graceful collision with the book shelf as he walked down the corridor that looked sparkling new and searched for the classroom number. His foolish feelings had been pushed aside by the reality of a new class that was about to start. He saw the room, spied a desk in back next to a window and sat down. The cool air-conditioning and his Schlitz from Kelly's had his arms turning into a pillow on the desk top. His head had no trouble finding the cushion, the Schlitz and picking up dead tree branches all day tugging on his drowsy eyes. He heard the desk next to him scrape ever so gently on the dark tile floor and his eyes reluctantly opened. It was her. His preppie ship that had passed him in the early evening with the sweetest, *Bye* he had ever heard was now docked next to him. She smiled, crossed her legs, and one of her cordovan penny loafers suddenly dangled from the toes of her left foot. The preppie ship's rigging and classic lines drove him nuts. It was like Millicent Krenz had jumped into his life after so many times of ignoring his nervous requests to ask her to dance at eighth grade boy-girl parties. His horny adolescent mind was once again creating the ultimate female companion in a euphoric romantic setting complete with erotic sex that would hospitalize most humans. But he wasn't a teenager now.

He sat up, mumbled something about a nap before class made his mind more alert and smiled back at her. There was a nod in her direction, his eyes still half closed and he repeated his sheepish, "Hi" again. There was her matching, "Hi," and a, "Do you mind if I sit here?"

Georgie sat up, sliding his desk closer to the window until the wall stopped it. He gave several head movements complete with a facial expression that said, "Please," in a thousand ways. He could hear Nana Beam say, "Giorgio, bella figura."

He knew it was bad manners to stare, but he couldn't take his eyes off of her. He tried, but not very hard. William Shakespeare may have been the topic of his next to last class, but all he could concentrate on was catching sneak peeks at this preppie Juliet who had entered his life. He knew little to nothing about *Romeo and Juliet*, and even less about Shakespeare but, he was sure Romeo's love didn't wear penny loafers. He was also convinced that Shakespeare and Romeo never got a glimpse, several glimpses, of the shapeliest calf he had seen since starched petticoats and his first glance at Patrice's legs. Then class began and that's when he noticed it. His heart began to sink at the dock. She was taking notes in, of all things, short hand, her ball point pen shooting out royal blue curly-cues across the first page of her spiral secretary's notebook. "Short-hand," he said to himself, feeling more depressed by the second, "The broad's got to be a damned genius. I bet her GPA is a perfect four point zero." Several more glances had him thinking, "I bet she comes from money." He took another peek. "Looks like she stepped out of the window of Marshall Field's," he thought. His thoughts continued to explode. "The chick's out of my league. Brains, beauty and bucks," he repeated to himself. Then he reined in his overactive mind and cut off the conversation he was having with himself with one simple statement. "You're married, dip-shit."

The first class session was coming to an end and he couldn't believe it. "Already?" he muttered, experiencing a first in his academic life. He shook his head, blinked and said aloud, "Wow!"

"Wow?" she repeated, a quizzical look accompanying her question.

He felt sheepish and tried not to look at her. "Wow as in one down and not quite as big a bunch to go." His explanation was followed by a sigh bordering on exhaustion. Then he added, solely for his own benefit, "And another step along the primrose way into the everlasting bonfire has come to an end." He didn't see her smile as he watched the frumpy professor, her frizzy bun tilted about twenty degrees off the center of her head, stack her yellow tinged notes. Her half lens reading glasses looked as if they were about to slip off her nose as she put away her papers into a brown, beat up leather brief case with two straps, the buckle missing from one. His arms went out to both sides in a stretch as he yawned; his left hand just missed hitting her in the face. "Oh, god, I'm sorry," he said, apologizing all over himself. "You must think I'm the world's biggest loser."

"No you're not," she said, in a whisper coated with a smile, her foot sliding back into her penny loafer. "If anybody thought you were a loser, it would be William Shakespeare for thinking this class was that bad." She folded her stenographer's notebook, gave a click of her ball point pen and the evidence of her being a student disappeared into her purse. "I think the Bard of Avon would approve of how our professor presented her interpretation of some of the works she covered tonight."

"She covered more than one of his works tonight?" he asked,

his eyes now fully open and feeling incredibly foolish. "Where was I?" He knew exactly where he had been when he heard her reply.

"I was snoring?" he repeated.

She nodded and then smiled a smile that began to melt his heart. "Then, when you weren't snoring, you were mumbling in your sleep." She paused and looked at him in a questioning way. "Something about going to a wake or funeral or something like that," she said. Then unable to keep a lid on her curiosity she asked, "Who is Nana Beam?"

"I didn't," he said, trying to find a way not to come across as a total idiot; recalling one of his father's pearls about bringing disrespect to the family. "Nana Beam's my grandmother," he said. He paused and didn't know why he said what he said next. "She's my idol."

"That's so sweet," she said, her head indicating a slight nod.

He saw her smile and his heart trembled like his father's fingers on the Tribune.

"You'll have to tell me all about it sometime," she said, curiosity accompanying another nod and a smile.

Her smile made his heart tremble even more, and she said, "As for your snoring, "I believe that came during the quote about fate our professor gave from *Julius Caesar*."

"I was talking about wakes in my sleep?" he asked, his head going from side to side, a dumb look on his face. "Julius Caesar?"

Her smile obliterated her nod.

His heart stopped trembling and began to melt.

"Wakes?" he asked again.

Her smile seemed to swallow her face.

"You mean we also covered Julius Caesar tonight?" he asked, his statement matching the look on his face.

"And then some," she said, her head now going from side to side, enhancing her smile.

"Well," he said, finding his opening to make himself not look like a he was totally brain dead, "she's better than many I've had here." He thought he had sounded like a seasoned professional student until another yawn came out of him and he knew his wife's appraisal of him had been more than accurate. As he pulled his arms in for a second embarrassing time, he began rubbing his temples with his thumbs while shutting his eyes as tight as he could. Then he opened them and said, "I'll get Romeo and Juliet down after I re-read my notes."

She looked at the top of his desk, a blank page of his notebook looking back and then gave him a questioning look. "Is that your after-the-lecture survival routine?" she asked.

"You mean, almost punching the person next to me in the face," he said, feeling himself turning red.

"Not that," she said, appearing to enjoy the wall of flames creeping up his cheeks. "It's the way you massaged your temples."

"Just a habit," he said, not realizing that a pair of thumbs digging into the side of one's head with rapid circular motions was normal. He gave a shrug and got up from his seat. "Guess I'll have to buy the books for this class." He looked at her enthralled at what he saw and knowing that Nanna Beam disapproved.

"If you'd like, I'll give you a copy of my notes when we meet the day after next," she said, turning into a concerned, helpful fellow student.

He started to blush all over again knowing that he hadn't jotted down a single word, not even the professor's name. "Thanks." Then not knowing why, he asked her, "Which way are you headed?" The question had just left his lips and he wanted to take it back. It was innocent enough; very general; almost vague. She could live in three other directions than his northerly route to West Rogers Park. The odds for her refusing his offer were in his favor.

"North," she replied.

Accepting his loss, he decided to be polite, to be a nice guy. "Me too," he said, thinking it wouldn't go any further and quickly tossing in the distance restrictions. "I live in Rogers Park, off of McCormick." He could still see her eyes shine; hear her voice; the sweet sound of music.

"I live in Evanston," she said.

The oft learned family lessons were being tested, and he could see the pearls rolling off the frayed end of a broken string along with the rattling of Rosary beads. "Right next door," he commented. Then, without a pause, "Would you like a ride? I mean if you don't have a car or if you haven't driven here or..." He caught himself stammering and stuttering like he was in the eighth grade talking to Millicent Krenz on the phone for the first time.

"I'd love a ride," she said, as they started toward the classroom door. "The CTA has been known to be a real pain at times, especially waiting at Howard for the Linden train."

They walked several blocks to where he had found his day's lucky parking space, the three blocks being a gift from the parking gods. "Hope you had your shots," he joked, referring to the rusted out beater of a Chevy he laid claim to, embarrassed for the first time in front of his one and only new female passenger ever. The ride north was only a ride and, in his rationalizing mind, a nice gesture on his part. He took Fullerton east to the Outer Drive, the lake breeze whipping through the open windows fanning away almost all of the evidence of a faulty muffler and rusted exhaust pipe. He wanted to enjoy the innocence of chauffeuring around a preppie pin-up girl, but couldn't, not with the other passengers in the car; those being the pictures in his mind of a pregnant wife and a baby daughter at home. He sensed a black cat prowling back and forth over the junk of his notebook and work clothes in the back seat, the cat purring and saying smugly, "Between us there are nine lives. Guess who has the nine?" He dropped her off in front of her apartment never hearing of Hinman and quickly drove off with another, *Bye*, swinging west on the next block in a trail of light blue smoke. Then he turned south on Asbury wanting more than ever to get home.

* * * * *

His second class session had ended and he found himself turning and saying to Maggie Stephenson, "Need a ride?" He found himself quickly spinning away fearing that she wouldn't.

"A ride would be appreciated," she said, sounding polite, appreciative and with a touch of eagerness.

He didn't see her smile, is head bent down as he pretended to check the floor around him to see if he had all of his belongings. They walked the three blocks again to his car and he took the same route to the Outer Drive, Lake Michigan adding to the atmosphere and conversation that seemed to be dominated by Maggie Stephenson. He didn't care. What he did care about took place just as he pulled up to the curb in front of her apartment on Hinman. That care came in the shape of her question: "Would you like to come up for a glass of lemonade?"

"Ah," was all he managed to say.

"Squeezed it myself," she added, her voice coaxing.

"Giorgio," he heard his Nana Beam say. The way she said his name was all he had to hear. "Ah," he repeated. Then his hand went to the ignition and he switched it off. "Why not," he said, with a casual shrug that masked the panic in his chest. "Something cool sounds great."

It will be more than cool," she said, her car door opening up with a series of annoying, embarrassing creaks and squeaks . "It's been sitting in the ice box since this morning."

"Ice box," he repeated a cross between a smile and surprise across his face. "I haven't heard that description since I was a kid and heard my Nana Beam use it."

"That's the only thing I've ever heard it called," she said, then laughing. "I mean, what's a refrigerator?"

They both laughed.

He hesitated and wished he hadn't as her hand playfully landed on his and he slid the keys out of the ignition. At the same time he felt his heart stop, all feeling immediately vacating his body.

"I know it sounds terribly old fashioned," she said, sounding apologetic, "but I learned how to make lemonade from my grandmother back in Traverse City."

"That's in Michigan, isn't it?"

"It is," she said, pointing at the front entrance to the dark brick apartment building that was similar, but smaller, than the one where he lived. They were walking up to her front door. "Gram's secret was to add a pinch more sugar but leave the squeezed lemons in the pitcher," she explained.

He had forgotten what else she said as they climbed the stairs to the third floor landing, each step creating sounds that should have been in a spooky movie. She stopped in front of the oak door with one too many coats of carelessly applied varnish; fumbled with her key ring that was not quite the size of what the security guards at the Chicago Park District garage lugged around and bounced her hip against the door. Hot stifling air hit them. Then he took a step across Nana Beam's warning and heard Maggie Stephenson say, "It sticks when the weather gets hot and humid."

Georgie saw her give a nod at the heavy door and didn't move as he watched her head down the hall. He heard her say, "Be a dear and close the door." Then she disappeared down the hall into the kitchen at the back of the apartment. The windows in the apartment were open, but that didn't do any good. His short sleeve button down collar shirt and Chinos stuck to him as if they had been painted on with a coat of Elmer's glue. "Get your butt out of here," he muttered to the empty living room that looked like his mother and Nana Beam had a hand in furnishing it. Then he heard his Nana Beam. "Giorgio, you getta your *culo* outta dare now!" she said, without scolding him. Before he could obey Nana's order he saw the cause of the heat and humidity walking towards him, a tall glass in each hand, and he knew his butt wasn't going anywhere.

Chapter 6

Now it was March, almost thirty plus years later, and there was no lemonade in an ice filled glass. His Chinos, now made in Honduras, weren't blotting up his perspiration, only trying to keep his legs from freezing. There had never been a glass of lemonade in his life since. He was wearing his standard resurrected wake attire, navy blue blazer, Chinos, white button down collar shirt and a red and blue striped tie, the one he had purchased when he graduated from DePaul. His eyes glanced quickly around the room, thankful that he didn't recognize a soul. If he had, there would have been no way he could explain why he was there; not without lying and not without offending his Nana Beam who had always reminded him about telling the truth.

"Giorgio," she would begin, her loving eyes never able to be serious when she talked to him, the choppy Italian accent colliding with the broken English. "It's a sin to tell a lie."

He hated himself for having been a liar; lying to Nana Beam; trying not to lie to Maggie Louise Stephenson; then feeling and looking like the proverbial kid with his hand caught in the cookie jar when Maggie asked her simple gut wrenching question about whether or not he was married. He never forgot how she sobbed, how he held her and apologized until there were no more tears and apologies. He patiently shuffled along in a numb course to where she lay in state. Then he found himself next in line and dropping down on the kneeler, one knee down, the good one, and the football knee injury from St.

Pat's High School with the shredded ACL up. He made the sign of the cross, not believing, trying not to look at her. Time and finality couldn't hide her beauty. His index finger traced a tiny sign of the cross by the shirt button in front of his heart. "Bless me Father for I have…" He caught himself and hoped desperately that no one had heard his whispered prayer of making a Confession. That prayer was quickly abandoned and he said reverently, "Rest in peace, Maggie." He paused and remembered the last words he had ever spoken to her in person that night so long ago. "I'll always love you." Then there was an unfinished *Memorarie,* another quick sign of the cross and he gave a push on the arm rest, stood up with the accompaniments of both knees creaking and started to leave.

"Thank you for coming."

The words startled him and almost made him jump. Georgie turned and thought he was looking into a mirror, seeing a jaw in the reflection drop at the same time his did. He caught a glimpse of an extended hand and grasped it, relieved that he had a chance to calm himself inside and regroup. He desperately wanted to shut his eyes and jam his thumbs into his temples.

It was a cordial, sensitive handshake, the kind that happens only at wakes. "I'm George Stephenson," the image in the mirror said to him. "Maggie's son," he said, pride in his introduction.

He didn't know how to let go of the hand. "George Porter," he said, still grasping on to the hand of someone he didn't know, but felt he had known from the time he had met George Stephenson's mother.

"Where did you know my mom from?" George Stephenson

asked, his own hand still hanging on. "Did you teach with her? Were you one of her faculty members?"

He tried to formulate answers to simple questions without staring. He longed to hear Nana Beam's words, any words. His eyes found the faded flowery pattern of the dark worn carpet, the flowers appearing trampled on too many times much like his life. "Ah, no," he muttered. "I'm not a teacher. I was once. Worked with troubled kids," he rambled, unable to stop himself. "I work in the Recorder of Deeds Office now. Your mom and I went to school together way back when. That's when I worked for the city in the Forestry Department." He felt totally stupid for spilling out a capsule history of himself. Pausing, trying to stay calm, he was angry with himself for not turning around in the foyer earlier and making a mad dash into the frigid night for the parking lot. "It was summer school. De Paul University; Lincoln Park," he said, and then chopping off his words as his jaw snapped shut. He looked into the mirror of her son's eyes again and was reminded of how he looked when he first met Maggie. His hand slid free and he once again suppressed the urge to run when he heard his name repeated. "Did you say your name was George Porter?"

His head tried to nod, stopping after the downward half, feeling heavier than the tree stumps he remembered picking up and heaving into the back of the forestry truck he once drove. He thought he heard himself answer in the affirmative and then silently cursed himself for not turning and dashing from the chapel like some crazed maniac when he heard Maggie's son's next comment.

"My mom told me about a George Porter she once knew."

"Really," he said, acting surprised, his mannerisms projecting a tango of denial dancing across his face as beads of sweat popped up on his upper lip making him look like Nixon debating Kennedy on television decades earlier. "You mean there's more than one like me out there in the world?"

George Stephenson smiled. "That I don't know. I only know what she told me."

"And that was?" he asked, sounding way too guarded and glad that his sport coat hid the growing stains of sweat under his arms.

"She mentioned that the George Porter she knew would get testy when called Georgie. No offense, but you look kind of old to be a Georgie."

"No offense taken," he said, trying desperately to find a glimpse of light at the opening of his escape route, but finding total darkness and surprised that he was unable to stop talking. "Being called Georgie at my age would certainly tick me off."

There was more than a pleasant smile on George Stephenson's face as he continued to talk to Georgie, the line of well-wishers paying their last respects growing behind them. "I vaguely remember as a little guy the name Georgie being said to me by Mom. His hands slowly went to his temples and he began to massage them with his thumbs.

Georgie suddenly prayed for God, for anyone, to strike him dead. Along with his prayer, he tried to swallow and said, "Looks like you've had a long day."

"Even longer tomorrow," he said. There was an agreeing shake of the head. "Can you believe this is the first and only wake I've ever been to?"

Georgie could feel himself try to give some facial expression of understanding, but nothing he thought of made the connection from his brain to his face. "My parents used to take me to these things all the time," he said, wanting to stop, but unable to. "I grew to hate them." He cut himself off and started to apologize. "I mean, I don't hate paying my respects to your mother. Oh, God, hate wasn't a very good choice of words."

George Stephenson smiled back. "No apology necessary, Mister Porter," he said. He shifted gears as if nothing uncomfortable had just taken place. "The last time Mom mentioned George Porter was in the hospice just before she died."

He began to feel like the frightened comedy character in an old horror movie wanting to say, "Feet, do your stuff!" And, just like the character, eyes wide, mouth open, nothing coming out and feet unable to move, he took a quick inhale and his experiences at attending wakes kicked in. "My deepest sympathy to you and your family on the loss of your mother," he said. He reached out and patted George Stephenson's shoulder. It was one of those pats that said *I don't have the words to convey what I'm feeling so this is the next best thing I can do.* He knew that one of the things he could really do was to put all the distance he could between himself and the funeral home. This would be a wake he would remember until whoever the mourner or mourners might be who stood at the side of his own casket looked down and said: *Do you know we've got a secret too*? His image looked back at him, suddenly appearing sad and looking like a lost soul.

"Mom and I were what you would call family."

It was hard for him to hear her called, Mom. "Your dad?" he asked. His questioned echoed in his ears.

"I never knew him."

Georgie kept his mouth closed, his face trying to show that

he understood while he silently cursed himself for leaving the warmth and comfort of his living room in the house where he grew up. What he was now experiencing was something he never wanted to face again. He thought of his Nana Beam telling him so long ago when the warning went out after he and Millicent Krenz were seen entering her parent's dilapidated frame garage that looked like it was about to fall down. The neighbor giving the alert was only concerned that the two youngsters would get hurt. That neighbor and even Georgie's parents and Nana Beam had no idea that Millicent was going to let Georgie Porter feel her up.

Georgie felt her up. Then they got into an argument when a feel wasn't enough and his sky rocketing passion had him attempting to explore Millicent's southern hemisphere. She had tried to push his hand away saying, "No Roman hands and Russian fingers." He stayed insistent saying, "I'm Irish and Italian."

Millicent wasn't amused, slapped him and ran from the garage screaming, "Mother!" She told her mother; her story complete with tears, innocence and a halo that Georgie Porter had put his hands on her. For emphasis, she added a sniffle and pointed. Her mother marched to the Porter house and told Nana Beam who had answered the door.

Nana Beam's gestures; her looks of horror; the Italian words minus any signs of broken English lashed out at the air while she assured Millicent's mother that her grandson would feel the same sting of the lash as the Lord did at his Crucifixion. Then, face to face with her grandson, Nana Beam's words came out so lovingly they couldn't be ignored. "Giorgio, you never, never, never put your hands where they don't belong," she said, the never words ending in "a" sounds. "You no sin likea dat again," she warned. "Iffa you do, you paya for you sin." He never forgot those words, a divorce from Patrice and the loss of Maggie Stephenson were evidence of his payments.

The uneasy silence kept him talking. "I'm sorry. I just assumed your dad was alive or that your grandparents or relatives might be around."

"I do have my roommate, Max," he said, a touch of pride in his statement. He turned his head toward the sofa in front of the casket, the special seating arrangement for family members. "Mom really liked Max."

"There's a whole lot there to like," said Georgie trying not to sound flippant. "Is your friend a professional wrestler or something like that?"

George Stephenson smiled and shook his head. "Something like that," he said. He paused and looked at Georgie. Then out came a complete biography of Max Muldoon, defensive tackle, the NFL, and one of the first players to admit that he was gay. That statement came after two knees no longer worked along with one shoulder, a matching wrist, and an onslaught of arthritis had made it impossible for him to get out bed two days in a row after a game.

"I remember him," said Georgie, after listening to more of the biography of Max Muldoon who now ran his own floral shop that specialized in high end weddings. Max could do more than crush opposing ball carriers Georgie recalled. After he left football, his violence had been channeled into the love of floral arranging; that violence now crushing his competition in the floral business and made both straight and gay florists gawk in respectful awe. "He could move like greased lightning,"

Georgie interjected. "A guy carrying the ball opposite of where your roommate played never had the luxury to try and dance and fake out a tackler. Max hit him so hard there was an outline of the poor guy's body in the turf." Georgie smiled. "Crushed him like a bug."

Silence crept in again and Georgie, now seeing his opportunity to leave, patted George on the shoulder for what he hoped was a last time. "Again, my deepest sympathy to you," he said, the patented, worn, tried and true expression of condolence rolling off his lips. He thought for a second and added, "And to Max." His arm slid off George's shoulder and he patted his arm as his feet finally started to do their stuff.

"Look," Maggie's son said, sounding exactly like the responsible son that Georgie once tried to be, "there are all kinds of people here that I have to thank. You know my duty." He glanced at those waiting in line behind Georgie.

Georgie laughed catching the son by surprise.

"Did I say something funny?"

"Kind of," he said, unable to shake off the humor, explaining, "That's what my father taught me to say when he was preaching to me about my duty, respect for family, being responsible and reading the Irish Scratch Sheet." He saw the expression on George's face. "The obituary page," he said bringing clarity to his statement.

"I like that, George said. Then he became almost frantic. "The funeral's tomorrow, St. Athanasius Church in Evanston. It was my mom's favorite place to escape." The words were spilling from him. "She tried all of Evanston's Catholic churches: Nick's, Mary's and even Northwestern's...." He abruptly shut off the tap looking almost embarrassed, and swallowed hard. "If you can't make the funeral, maybe I could give you a call once this is all over." The tap popped open and his words were now gushing. "I'd like to talk to you more about my mom and maybe my dad. Mom said you might be able to clear up something for me. That is, if you're the George Porter she told me about." There was a nervous pause. "It's really important to me."

He never hesitated, reaching into his sport coat, pulling out a cheap ball point pen, and wrote his phone number on the first thing that resembled a piece of paper he could find. It was a remembrance holy card; the Blessed Mother kneeling in prayer on the front and an Irish toast on the back about, "May the wind be at your back." He had picked it up from the wooden stand that held the "Family and Friend's Book" he had signed. "Sure," he said, as he felt his feet beginning to cooperate more, "give me a call any time." Then, still ever the polite and respectful one, "Maybe we can get together for lunch; on me."

"That would be great." George Stephenson paused then said, "Lunch, however, isn't necessary, but it sounds like a great idea and it's on me."

"Yeah, great," Georgie said, trying to sound sincere while hiding his sense of relief that he would soon be outside in the blustery weather heading home. "Call me."

"I'll do that."

He didn't feel great as he found himself picking up several more memorial cards with Maggie's name as he exited the parlor trying not to run. The cards went into his jacket pocket and his pace quickened. An icy wind slapped him in the face not as playfully as how his Nana Beam would slap him on the cheek when she teasingly unloaded one of her pearls of philosophy on him.   He was oblivious to the wind as he retraced his path across the parking lot, making sarcastic comments to Mother Nature, motorists and any other living beings that he was pleased that the traffic on Skokie Boulevard gave him a break.   When he got to his car, it dawned on him that he was still carrying his coat over his arm.   He threw the coat onto the passenger seat and got in.   His hands choked the steering wheel, but the car wasn't going anywhere.   The key was in the ignition, engine still off, but his mind was firing on all cylinders.   He could see her son, looking like his son, their son.

Chapter 7

He didn't know how long he sat in his car before glancing at his bare hands wrapped around the steering wheel. They had turned blue. His feet felt numb. Then he saw his trench coat on the seat next to him seeming to say, "Giorgio, getta you head outta you culo before it freezes there." He turned on the ignition switch and then flipped on both the heater and defroster to high. More cold poured into the car, but he ignored his trench coat.

The heater fan whirled but couldn't keep up with his mind. He could never forget the beautiful guilt filled feeling of their love making that night so long ago. It was the one and only time they actually made love; both not wanting to stop. A combination of Mother Nature, human physiology and the *Kinsey Report* dictated otherwise. There had been the tell-tale warning that common sense was being replaced by agonizing pleasure. He wanted with all his heart to ignore the warning, to continue making love to her until he could never make love again. He knew the feeling, his senses screaming with pleasure urging him on. Then, at the last possible moment, he yelled out a warning to himself: "Stop!" At least he thought he had stopped in time. That was his intention. He always had good intentions when making love to Patrice, but she never wanted to stop, and he didn't. He knew the message; knew what was about to happen. The message had his body going into spasms, unintelligible moans replacing words of love that got locked up on his tongue. He could never forget how his climax seemed to last an eternity, his love being emptied on her midsection.

"Oh, God, dearest Maggie," he said, as the interior of his car listened intently while tiny gale swept ice pellets tried to penetrate his car. He made an attempt to adjust the heater and defroster to get the thin film of ice removed from inside his windshield, but the attempt was as far as he got. It was as if the final remains of Maggie Louise Stephenson, who he had nicknamed Aggie, were making him pay the price for violating their pledge not to see each other again after that last night. He had tried to honor the pledge, but ended up breaking his promise less than a week later. She didn't. His calls were met with a polite silence, and he was only able to get out the familiar, "Hi." That was followed with what sounded like a plea coming from him about wanting to see her. His plea received a click at the other end of the phone. There were more pleas and more clicks with her never saying anything besides an initial, "Hello." The one word sound of her voice had him experiencing momentary rapture. Then a click brought misery. He mailed her what seemed like a thousand letters, dropping one in the mail box, sometimes two, three, or even four every day. There was nothing in return, not even his letters. He sent dozens upon dozens of roses, the small cards jammed with tiny printing as he tried to squeeze in his message of love to her. The flowers and miniature messages continued until he couldn't afford them and then, knowing how she loved annual plants, he bought as many varieties he could find. He packed them in a homemade box he made with sheets of corrugated cardboard and enough packing tape to put Humpty Dumpty back together again and dropped off the huge box of plants inside the entrance to her apartment building as if the Postal Service had made the delivery. There was no response. His frustration became so great that one night he sat in his car for hours in sub zero weather in front of her apartment. About midnight she got out of a cab and he jumped out of his car and ran to her front door cutting her off. "I just had to see you," he said, his voice a combination of love, agony and desperation. She ignored him. He stood frozen as she walked right by him into her building as if he didn't exist. He never forgot the look she gave him knowing it was the result of an all-time dumbest of dumb tell-all love letters he had sent to her. He had penned the letter after consuming the better part of a bottle of Martin's VVO Scotch without using a glass. It was the last of the two bottles he found in the attic of the old house after his dad died. He got blind, stupid drunk and unloaded his stupidity telling Aggie about his pregnant wife, the birth of his second child, a son, how he couldn't sleep, didn't want to live, and wanted only her. She didn't want him. Patrice didn't want him either. Her love had died about the time the honeymoon ended and her husband's money went for tuition and not for her and life in a garden apartment became a reality. She finally filed for divorce.

His hand finally adjusted the defroster and the icy glaze began to disappear. He was shivering but not from the cold. The cat he envisioned in the back seat of his car so many years ago had been more than right. He never shook the feeling of being shunned by Aggie. Alone and lonely, he found himself in bars, his imaginary cat a constant companion placing claws in his tender hide, laughing at him, saying, "I told you one life was all you got." His reply was always a muttered, "Fuck off, pussy wussy." Sometimes his reply was too loud and a female patron seated at the bar near him took personal offense. He would apologize to the lady and eventually buy her a drink. His drink always came with more apologies and smooth small talk. Smooth turned to promises and the promises could fill a barrel of lies. Sometimes the lies resulted in sex. He didn't care. It didn't matter to Georgie where he got it. He figured he had gotten laid in every make and model of automobile to come off the assembly lines in Detroit, Asia and Europe. Front seat or back seat made no difference. The car's hood or trunk deck offered variety that the mechanical engineers' designs never imagined. There was sex in hallway entrances of various condos and apartments. There was sex up against her front door, inside her front door, on the floor with the front door open or closed. He didn't care. No matter how he tried he could never experience the same intense passion and love that he had felt that single night a million years ago with Maggie.

He eventually kept his fly zipped up, put the cork back in the bottle and renewed his efforts to find his preppie one more time. She had disappeared, moving from the Hinman address, her trail ending in thin air. He continued to sift through the frustrating thin air until he began turning against himself, telling his closest friends that if they ever wrote a book about ass holes, they should use his picture for the front cover. His friends never wrote that book, and then the Irish Scratch Sheet found her and he found someone who looked like him.

His thumbs found his temples and he pressed and rubbed. Then shouting to the empty interior of the car, "I'm going to lunch with someone who looks like he could be the fucking son I never knew I had!" He eased the car out of the parking lot convinced that George Stephenson was his son, and totally confused as to how. Fifteen minutes on the southbound Eden's expressway and another fifteen minutes or so navigating city traffic found him home. He sat in his living room, his body swallowed up by the worn out spongy easy chair that his father once lived in and tried to make sense out of what he had just experienced. He could picture his Nana Beam at the kitchen table making her gnocchi that were always too pasty soft for him, saying smugly with a touch of grandmotherly, "Didn't I a tell you abouta paying for you sins?"

He got up and went to the kitchen where he poured himself a Diet Coke, no ice, and questioned his sanity. "Why did you have to give him your phone number?" He reached in his shirt pocket and removed a half dozen or so holy cards, the ones he had taken on his way out of the funeral parlor after he had written down his phone number for George Stephenson. Suddenly his mind was back at De Paul that summer so long ago. He was in class again with Aggie, watching her ball point pen scribble the curly-cues of her shorthand, his own pen, as usual, idle. His brain, however, wasn't. He found himself quoting William Shakespeare. *Destiny gives us our choice–climb– or slip. She won't let us stand still. Men at some time are masters of their fates.*

He watched the bubbles of his Coke dance and fizzle before taking a sip. Feelings he didn't know existed wormed through his entire being. "It can't be," he muttered, the dancing popping bubbles that seemed to have gained added exuberance after absorbing his words. "I can't have," he said, not convincing the Coke, the glass, the empty kitchen or the memory of his Nana Beam. "Could it have happened?"

Then the freezing night he had waited for her in front of her apartment, the night she walked past him without saying a word, now made sense. The long, beige wool winter coat she wore that night had done its job, hiding her condition from him. It didn't register back then, her face fuller under the matching wool stocking cap, and the coat unable to conceal a stomach that was growing. She didn't hate him after all. She was just being Maggie the thoughtful; Maggie the intelligent; Maggie who would never hurt even a fly; not even Patrice who she didn't know. Now he had another reason why he loved Maggie Stephenson from Traverse City, Michigan. She knew how to keep a secret.

Chapter 8

Her Little Secret

She felt the wet warmth of him on her tummy; so much of him; more than the teaspoon full she had read about. She had heard his words, believed each vowel, each consonant, cherishing every syllable. She believed him and knew in her heart that he loved and worshiped her. She loved the way he looked at her, how he adored her.

They both knew they were going to make love that night. There had been so many other nights where they came close, but always stopping, both feeling relieved that their relationship hadn't been consummated. Then it happened; their going away present to one another; after, there was his tender apology about making a mess on her, uttered when he thought she was sound asleep. She heard him quietly get out of bed and head for the bathroom; heard the water running. She knew he would return with a wash cloth and a towel.

Her hand found the nectar of his love and she swirled that part of him around her middle finger, coaxing it to where she wanted it to be, repeating the process several more times, wanting to be sure, then stopping when she heard him returning to the bedroom. She pretended to sleep, stirring as the warm wash cloth cleansed the remainder of their love making from her. He dried her and then kissed the newly cleaned area, repeating his soft words of love to her. Again he was gone. She could hear him in the bathroom, wanted to call to him, but knew that would violate their pact. Their love had been a secret and so would the finality of it. The effects of the drinks had more than relaxed her and she was careful not to move as he stood by the edge of the bed. He was fully clothed now, looking at her the way she loved to be looked at. His hand reached down and caressed her left ring finger, his words a whisper, "God, I want you forever." She didn't move even though she longed to hold him. Then she heard him crying. In what seemed like an agonizing eternity, there was the sound of him walking softly out of the room followed by the gentle click of the front door closing, this time without a tug and slam. He was gone and only then did she call out to him, "Georgie, I'll always love you." Her hands slid between her legs preventing the smallest drop from escaping. She sighed, "Georgie, you will always be a part of me." She could feel the Brandy Stingers continue to work on her beginning to bring on a tranquil, peaceful sleep. "Remember your favorite class?" she asked to a departed Georgie. *"Give thy thoughts no tongue,* is what Shakespeare said in Hamlet. Remember?" A warm, gentle smile caressed her because she knew he didn't. "Tonight," she said the word barely able to pass her lips. There was a drowsy pause, her eyes fully shut and the Stingers about to pull the covers over her, "Tonight is going to be my little secret."

PART IV
Trading Prushka

Wrigley Field
Circa 1951

Chapter 1

"For its one, two, three, strikes you're out,
At the old ball game."

The disastrous late spring of 1951 ranked as the absolute worst time of Gil Bauer's life. Well, perhaps it was the second worst time of his life. Having to live with the name *Gilead* affixed to his birth certificate took the grand prize. When he factored in taunts from his playmates and school classmates using obscene rhyming couplets to ridicule him, he despised his name even more.

His grandfather, Poppy Paul straightened out Gil's life and his name when he reached the border between ages six and seven. Once, after the weekly Sunday chicken dinner at Gil's grandparent's massive brownstone home in Humboldt Park, a place that fascinated Gil, Poppy Paul said to him: "You got a good name. It means 'mountain'."

Gil admired, as well as feared, no person in the world more than his Poppy Paul. His eyes locked onto his grandfather's almost sinister brown eyes ringed with a hint of a halo. He gave a respectful nod that was barely a twitch. When his grandfather spoke Gil listened; in fact, everyone at the huge, rectangular black walnut dining room table listened. The table looked like it may have come over on the Mayflower, or even preceded that crossing.

Poppy Paul had been an officer in the Prussian Army during World War I, but his stature didn't show it. The joke around

Gil's house with his father was that his father-in-law had to sit on a Chicago phone directory so he could see his plate on the dinner table. Gil's father often remarked, "Who did the little shit fight, midgets?" He never said it to his father-in-law's face. The moment the combatants signed the Armistice ending World War I, Gil's grandfather fled Europe to America with his young bride who was several months pregnant.

"Your name comes from the Bible," Poppy Paul told his grandson. "Gilead is a mountain that overlooks the Jordan. Near my homeland we have the Carpathian Mountains. I see you as big and strong like those mountains."

Poppy Paul's love of central Europe and his homeland remained strong, like the tempered steel of his officer's saber he had carried with pride and doubt. The doubt part consisting of that tempered steel blade fending off an enemy's bullet.

Gil would sneak a look at the saber after dinner when his grandfather was, as Poppy Paul termed it, "resting mein eyes" while being swallowed up by his massive Chesterfield chair. "Don't let those friends of yours make fun of you," his grandfather would say, his words like orders coming from a Prussian officer to his troops. "They're spineless little blobs of *shite* with no brains. A good kick in the arse is what those dumbkopfs need," he said, making sure that he emphasized the dual description of Gil's friends. "And you should be the one doing the kicking."

"But, Poppy Paul my parents always told me to turn the other cheek."

"Your ass has two cheeks. You get a kicked in one and then a kicka in da other. How many times do you like getting kicked?"

"But Poppy Paul," Gil said politely, without breaking eye contact.

"No buts," said Poppy Paul. If you want buts, kick their butts. That'll shut the little poopecks up," his grandfather said, coining one of his favorite expressions; all of those centered on or near the human body's excretory functions.

Chapter 2

Kicks in the backside had nothing to do when Gil's world started to crumble. His doomsday officially began during the last week in April to be exact; another major league baseball season underway with the New York Yankees guaranteed to win the American League pennant, the New York Giants and the Brooklyn Dodgers doing battle in the National League.

Gil's Armageddon started innocent enough when he stepped into the batter's box, its outline etched into the street that was Marmora Avenue. The etching tool was a small chunk of flag stone temporarily removed from its position sculpting the front walk of Leone's two flat brownstone. He tapped his nicked up bat on the manhole cover in the middle of the street that was home plate. The tar intersection of the street, butting up against each curb, served as first and third bases. A larger chunk of flag stone, again courtesy of an unknowing Leone family, was second base and quickly removed from play when a car would speed toward their game. A final adrenaline induced tap on the iron sewer cover added another dent in the top of the pocked marked bat. The game was on the line. Gil had fouled off the first two pitches, one going into the Mulchrone's rock garden that consisted of mostly dandelions trying to touch the sky and buried in their Yews. That particular foul ball caused a game delay while the ball got fished out with the aid of several similar scarred baseball bats poking and prodding the reluctant ball back into play. The second foul ball, a long fly that bounced off the front of the Braunschwiger's house, sent the players scurrying in every direction shouting, "No chips!" The ball's long, slow arc curved toward the ornate, leaded glass front window just coming up short of the window and careening off an ornate cement ledge. They all breathed easier as they jogged back to their respective positions on the street. Each player avoided shortcuts that would take them across a front lawn or a grassy parkway to their positions out on the street. Playing on a neighbor's front lawn, or even walking on it, was prohibited by a self-imposed set of arbitrary rules, its articles of fair play and sportsmanship tied loosely to parental threats to respect neighbor's property; most of the threats accompanied by a hand suggesting that a swat to the backside of one's head would follow. In Gil's case, his father's warning was more like a death threat. "Keep off the O'Malley's goddamned lawn if you know what's good for you." His father would return to tending to his own small plot of grass that he cherished and added. "I don't want that pig shit Irish bastard telling me that my idiot son stomped the crap out of his front lawn because he forgot what a sidewalk was used for."

The game continued with each player relieved knowing that he wouldn't have to chip in to pay for a new window and that the unlucky batter wouldn't have to face the wrath of Chuckie Braunschweiger. He was an only child who was a mean spirited pudgy lad all of four foot eleven, but thought and acted like he was seven foot six. Chuckie had one mood and that was nasty. When the kids on Marmora Avenue saw him they sprinted through gangways and alleys, their articles of fair play quickly being forgotten as they raced for safety. Chuckie had his own rule book, that containing only one article, and that article stating, *Thou Shalt Kick the Crap Out of Those Who Are Deserving*. None of them waited around to see how deserving they were.

Gil dug in the soles of his PF Canvas Flyers, as well as any tennis shoe could be dug into cement, and cocked his bat. He made sure he stood exactly like his Cubs' hero, Andy Pafko. The third pitch floated in like a giant lazy balloon, the brand name on the ball visible from a city block away. Gil's eyes grew as big as the ball. This was his pitch. It had victory written all over it. This was his time. Hero worship waited. His muscles tensed. He whipped his bat around in a swing mightier than the legendary Casey's and missed. Then he swung again and missed, and yet again, striking out. It was the longest strike out in baseball history and the players on both teams were rolling around on the street in various states of convulsive laughter. He walked from home plate trying to ignore the laughter and not believing that he saw Andy Pafko grinning while giving him a wink. Gil was dragging his Louisville Slugger along the cement street behind him. The bat weighed considerably more than when it came off the assembly line. At least a pound of nails held the cracked handle together and the nail heads were covered with approximately two miles of black electrician's friction tape for safety. Now Gil understood how Mighty Casey and all of Mudville felt.

That memorable, unique strike out couldn't begin to compare with what was in store for him. The next three pitches he would face that spring couldn't have been tougher if Bullet Bob Feller, Prince Hal Newhauser and Back-to-Back No Hit Johnny Van der Meer had combined their talents on each pitch.

The first pitch was hurled at him the next week during the St. Ferdinand grammar school eighth grade outing to Riverview, the grandiose and magical amusement park at Belmont and Western. A group of soon-to-be-male-graduates brand new to adolescence and complete with raging hormones and minimal brain functions, had concocted a plan to cop a feel from the girl of their choice. According to their plans, the feel would be copped while riding the Bobs roller coaster. A major part of their plan, roughly ninety nine percent, included the selected female classmate nestled next to each boy, his protective arm draped over a soft, tender shoulder. The plan's critical layout had the individual hand hanging down far enough so that it was in line with an unsuspecting boob. According to Gil's best friend, Bus Brasen who was the class clown, self-proclaimed expert on all things sex and budding mad scientist, physics his specialty, centrifugal force would do the copping. That was Brasen's plan and they all bought into it after hearing him explain: "You let your hand hang there by the bulge in her sweater. When the Bob's goes into one of those tight turns the force is going to flop your mitt right on her tit." Brasen laughed himself silly before saying, "Mitt on a tit. Get it? I'm a poet and I don't know it."

Who they picked as the recipient of their cop would come by either default or the luck of, or not so luck of, the draw. The selected female designates, also brand new to adolescence, would also, the males secretly hoped, have the same or greater hormonal activity pulsating through their sensuous bodies, the evidence of buds just starting to bloom. The simplicity of the male plan, like their collective mentalities, was to both tease and coax the girls to ride the giant roller coaster. The question was how creative would the teasing and coaxing have to be so that each would pair up with that girl of their fantasy and not end up riding the Bobs alone like they usually did or seated with one of the B.V.M nuns who would be chaperoning the trip.

Ushering the girl of their choice into a seat on the giant roller coaster didn't appear to be a problem, at least not according to Brasen. He was held in high esteem by his classmates for having removed a small brown paper bag from his father's dresser drawer and bringing it to school during lunchtime recess. The bag contained a collection of illustrated pornographic joke books called, *Eight Pagers*. After Brasen had shared his discovery with every eighth grade boy in the playground, he could do no wrong. Brasen's word, on all subjects related to life, liberty and the pursuit of happiness, was gospel and his Bible consisted of eight glorious and holy pages in a half dozen or so volumes. Whether Brasen preached, shared his knowledge of pin-up girls, pornography or the ups and downs of the male appendage, he could do no wrong.

Gil and the others were in awe at how well endowed the genitalia of the cartoon characters were displayed, Brasen, boldly saying, "Mine's like that," the gap between his buck teeth hissing air with laughter. Later, as they discussed their roller coaster plan, Bus said to the guys around him, passing out his strategy for getting their special girl to be next to them on the Bobs, "Goose her. She'll be in that car faster than greased lightning."

There was no evidence of goosing. Crude, sometimes brute like shoves that would have made them eligible to go directly from St. Ferdinand's School to South Bend, Indiana to play football for Our Lady under the Golden Dome accomplished their goal. That is, except for Whizzer Wisnowski the smallest boy in the class at just under four foot nine inches. Whizzer had shoved Becky Gatz so hard he knocked her over and out the other side of the rollercoaster's car, his momentum, according to Brasen's physics, carrying him with her. A pimply faced, seventeen year old attendant and ticket taker with a greasy, black pompadour and a cigarette pack rolled up under the sleeve of a faded white t-shirt quickly escorted Whizzer and a sobbing Becky off the ride.

Snuggling close to the object of one's affection appeared to be automatic as the protective security bar snapped shut locking both parties into the seat. That part of the plan, each male felt, had gone better than expected. That is, except for Gil. He had waited on the wooden platform for the Bobs to appear, suspended somewhere between a nervous breakdown, cardiac arrest, a pending erection, and figuring how he would tell Father White in confession on that next Saturday that he had sinned at Riverview Park. One thing hampered Gil's master plan besides his trying to dissuade a growing erection to have some patience. He was surrounded by what appeared to be every eighth grader in his school and they were blocking his plan of attack route. Also in his way, sprinkled strategically among his eighth grade class, were the unmistakable sinister, black silhouettes of the nuns all but blocking out the sun as well as his view of the girl who would, he hoped, thrill to his touch or as Brasen so succinctly put it, "One brush of your hand on her booby and she'll be your sex slave for life." Besides being surrounded by an enemy who he thought would have given his Poppy Paul a battle, brushing up against his right arm was the girl of his dreams and his impending sin. The reason for his sexual fantasies and nocturnal emissions was standing next to him, looking at him and smiling.

Before Gil knew it, the approaching roller coaster, wheels screeching, came to a stop. An open car was directly in line with his love object's right hip. Gil all but assured himself of a football scholarship to the University of Notre Dame by pushing tiny Judalyne Louis into the vacant car, quickly pinning her in. The crafty spider was next to his fly and he knew that the God's of Roller Coasters were with him. They weren't and that was part of his first strike, a fast ball, high and tight, aimed at the center of his forehead. The Gods of Roller Coasters had also hurled a pitch, another high fast one, at the passengers who were seated behind him. As the roller coaster made its second serious plunge, Judalyne was screaming and pressing herself against his side so tight he thought he felt something he had always wanted to feel. He had waited for what seemed like going through the eighth grade six times for that glorious moment to feel his fingers cup Judalyne Louis's boob with or without Brasen's theory of centrifugal force assisting him. Now that moment had arrived. The long, agonizing, patient wait had brought two unexpected bonuses. First, her screams had him being called on to be her knight in shining armor, to protect his fair damsel from the perils of further plunges and to ride off into the sunset on his changer with her in his arms while the Sons of the Pioneers sang, *Happy Trails to You*. This is what his nocturnal emissions had prophesied. The second, and last of his bonuses, was that the harder she pressed against him, the more madly in love he became and life couldn't be better. He was not only copping a feel, but centrifugal force had her copping a feel from him. At least that's what he thought as another scream from Judalyne begged him for his protection. Gil's mind quickly left a measly copped feel in the setting sun with the Sons of the Pioneers. There was another tight turn and Judalyne squeezed. Then she screamed. Gil couldn't believe what was happening as Judalyne squeezed and screamed, then squeezed and screamed again. Then the screams intensified along with an absence of squeezes. The screams continued, but the squeezes now switched to slaps. At first Gil thought he was dreaming. Then Judalyne's right hand swung across her body and landed on Gil's nose. He saw stars. Then he heard the words that all boys at his age dreaded. "I'm telling my father!" Gil then felt Judalyne's other hand tear at his hair. He was glad he had put an extra shake of Vaseline hair tonic on that morning before leaving for Riverview. The added lubricant had Judalyne's hand slipping off his hair. His feeling of glad lasted only a second. That's when Judalyne shifted her grabbing and went to clawing, latching on to Gil's cheek. He felt her finger nails trace four angry line from below his eye to his chin. "What did I do?" he shouted at her, as his dreams of getting more than what Bus told him he would get vanished into a trade for pain. He felt Judalyne shift to the opposite side of the car and didn't care. Just after she put as much distance from him that the dimensions of the car would allow, the Gods of Roller Coasters tested Gil's skills at the plate to see if he was up to handling their version of a high fast one. The Bobs went into a combination plunge, whipping turn, steep climb and final death defying dive. His Louisville Slugger and vanished erection were of no help. Not only did he whiff on the pitch, but the hot dogs he had inhaled earlier in the, who-could-eat-the-most-the-fastest contest with Bus Brasen were, in their own sadistic way, hurled from him. The contest's contents soared high above the intersection of Belmont and Western until gravity joined up with wind velocity. Some of the barely digested chunks rode the blustery west wind toward Lake Michigan while most of the more liquid and lighter contest remnants sailed up and back endearing him forever to the riders in the cars behind him and enshrining him into Riverview's Hall of Fame. He wanted to leap out of the car before it stopped, escaping every living and stationary thing behind and below before an onslaught of angry hands could pull him from the Bobs and end his times at bat for eternity. An army of his fellow knights wouldn't be able to save him from the mutilation he would surely face. The only good thing about his regurgitating all over Riverview Park was that Judalyne never saw or felt any of it. Her face was buried so tightly against the opposite side of the car she never saw his head go right and back. All of Riverview Park would later tell her.

Strike two came without him having taken the bat off his shoulder. Physically recovering from the Bob's ride at Riverview took about as long as it did to empty the contents of his stomach. Enduring the harassment of the guys for what was known as the Gil the Gagger episode didn't take much longer, ending the next day, the conclusion officially logged in during the Offertory of the six o'clock Mass. That's when Brasen tripped while carrying the two cruets filled with the water and wine. The word quickly spread through school how Bus went flying and then lay prone at the feet of the pastor, Fr. Dave Gwinn and too embarrassed to get up. Bus may have turned the color of Fr. Gwinn's red vestments lying sprawled out in front of the altar, but that didn't come close to how Gil felt each time he saw Judalyne who spun like a top, turning and quickly heading in the other direction every time she saw him. But those two events were only the start of the pitcher's wind up leading to strike two for Gil as the month of May began.

He had been walking the straight and narrow path since Riverview and not wanting to experience the reaction of his parents after they had found out. It was Brasen's mother who told his mother and it was his mother who told his father who accused his son, as well as all of his eighth grade classmates, of not having one complete brain between them. His accusation was accompanied by a swat that rearranged Gil's brown, Vaseline reinforced pompadour thanks to a nifty covering of his head with his hands. His mother's intervention prevented the further rearranging of his anatomy where, he sincerely believed, his eyes would have ended up peering out of his rectum. His Poppy Paul sat on the living room sofa violating his mother's edict of: "The living room is for company only." His head barely went from side to side while he muttered, "Dumbkopf," along with several other German words that Gil knew were not part of the orders his Poppy Paul used to order his men at the western front.

For historical accuracy, it is noted that Bus Brasen was the pitcher winding up and that strike two was a sucker pitch, the biggest unsportsmanlike, rule breaking strike in the recorded annals of the national pastime. The sucker pitch also destroyed every single article in their Rule Book. Loosely condensed, the violation read, *Thou Shalt Not Snitch*. That second strike two took place on Monday afternoon, the first school day of May; the month of Our Lady the mother of Jesus. May was also the month when all nuns actually used the beads they wore hanging to the floor from around their waist for prayer instead of a possible weapon against most of the male students. The males excluded from a bead flogging were those who said they might want to attend the seminary after they graduated.

As they entered school after the lunch recess, Brasen informed Gil that he was carrying a garter snake in his baseball cap, a battered blue creation with a hand-painted *C* on the front crown. The artistic letter supposedly represented Brasen's allegiance to the Cubs. The *C*, however, looked as if it had tipped over looking like a perfect *U*. Brasen's plan was to let the snake out of his cap as they were all kneeling saying the rosary to pay homage to the Blessed Mother. Gil couldn't believe what Brasen was about to do, but after he took a second look at his pal; he could see a definite resemblance between him and Jonathan in *Arsenic and Old Lace*. Gil knew he was doomed and no mountain range, not the Carpathians, the Alps or the Rockies had the strength to prevent that from happening. Fate, along with the alphabetical seating chart that nuns kept, had him kneeling to the immediate right of Brasen. He was going to be fingered as the disrespectful culprit or, at the very least, a sacrilegious accomplice and his graduation cake with the butter cream frosting and strawberry filling would lie rotting in the window of Koening's German Bakery on Addison Street. It was guilt by association and he knew he didn't have a prayer. Even being shielded in front from the all-seeing eyes of Sister Mary Bonito Gardini by the Grogan twins, Buddy the stutterer and Jimmy Joe who had already been accepted at Quigley Prep Seminary, couldn't help Gil. There wasn't a nun alive, surely not the rotund nun who had been irreverently named after a professional wrestler of the same name by the boys, would have taken sides with Gil and Bus after the garter snake, the size of an Anaconda, had been released during the praying of the rosary. Brasen wasn't one for waiting. His worn baseball cap he normally kept in his back pocket while in school was gripped in his right hand next to his right knee on the worn, highly polished tile floor. In his left hand was his rosary, minus approximately one third of the beads. No one noticed at first when the giant snake slithered out onto the worn light brown tile floor halfway through the first Hail Mary of the first decade. Brasen had figured the disruption would put an end to any prayers for that day and save his knees from the painful ordeal of the power of prayer.

Buddy Grogan was the first to see the snake and let out a string of staccato *S* and *H* combinations until the word, shit could finally be formed. His brother Jimmy Joe, a nickname his friends had given him since his mother always referred to him as Saints James and Joseph, began beating his breast with the closed fist of his right hand muttering something repeatedly in Latin before wetting himself. The girls began to shriek and holler, their screams drowning out Buddy and Jimmy Joe, as rosary beads flew through the air and razor sharp, respectful rows of the kneeling faithful in blue jumpers and white blouses stampeded for the door ignoring the statue of the Blessed Mother standing solemnly in the corner. Sister Mary Bonito Gardini showed no emotion and never missed a bead on her rosary. She walked devotedly to where the serpent was coiled up in front of the Blessed Mother's statue, reached down; her wrinkled hand barely visible from the sleeve of the black habit; grabbed the serpent behind the head and gave a blurring flick of her wrist. Somewhere between Buddy Grogan's stuttering strings of *shits* and, *blessed is the fruit of thy womb*, the snake became a piece of limp spaghetti. Sister then walked toward the third floor classroom window, a look of exaltation on her face for having dispatched one of Satan's shock troops back to the fires of Hell. The snake disappeared out the window free falling three stories to the landscaped ground below. None of the boys breathed knowing they, innocent or guilty, could be next. All eyes stayed glued on Sister as she made a simple gesture to the girls with her now serpent-less hand. The girls untangled themselves from the stacked pile of assorted limbs that had been created as they all tried to climb out of the room at the same time through the transom above the door. Obediently and devoutly, they silently returned to kneeling on the tile floor in three neat, but slightly shaken rows, traces of fear still visible on their faces.

After the rosary, Gil, Brasen, and the usual suspects, except Buddy and Jimmy Joe, who had been excused to go to the Boy's Room without first holding up one finger, were rounded up. They were systematically taken out to the hall one-by-one to be interrogated for committing one of the greatest of crimes against humanity since the Crucifixion. They all played dumb which wasn't far from playing. Brasen had the Gaul to finger Gil and Gil fingered him right back. Together they stayed after school filling two chalk boards with, *A sore hand is what I get for disrespecting the Mother of God, harming one of God's creatures and being a tattle tale*. Both Brasen and Gil were thankful that their parents weren't called to the convent knowing that if they had been their fathers would've transformed their necks so that they both looked like the snake after undergoing whiplash.

The *Break The Snakes Fuckin' Neck* incident, as Brasen proudly called it, did get Judalyne to finally stop avoiding Gil. She came up to him the next day during the lunch recess period where he stood talking to his friends in the school's play ground and emphatically said to him: "You're disgusting and I never want to see you again."

Her words didn't faze Gil. Time was on his side and he figured he still had a chance with her. His chance was quickly vaporized when she stood on her toes and managed to get her right index finger within six inches of his nose and the still visible scratches on his cheek from Riverview. He knew the romance was over after she had warned him by the following saliva sprayed statement: "If you even look in my direction again, I'm going to tell my father what you did to me on the Bobs." Judalyne may have been a petite four foot eleven but Mr. Louis, her father, was eleven foot four, and with the exception that he was white and not black, resembled the heavy weight champion Joe Louis. Gil had no desire to encounter the Brown, A.K.A. White Bomber and his lethal punches for copping a feel, throwing up all over Riverview Park or both. The next time he saw her was a brief glimpse as she came out the front doors of St. Ferdinand's Church after graduation. He never saw her again. Her words and rejection of him hurt for about a day. Hurting even more was Brasen's sucker pitch, the rat ball Gil had later called it, whizzing by his head high and tight and being called a strike. Gil still felt there was hope since he still had a strike to go.

Chapter 3

It was the first day of June, and Gil was well over mourning the loss of Judalyne when he and Brasen decided to celebrate their graduation from grammar school by going fishing in Lake Michigan. They had taken the CTA bus to the end of the line and then walked across the north end of Lincoln Park heading for the Horseshoe at Montrose Harbor. They pulled their fishing tackle, bait and lunch in a wobbly two wheel wire shopping cart that Bus had borrowed from his mother without her permission. Once on the concrete breakwater that resembled a giant question mark without the dot, they picked a spot at the very top of the Horseshoe and began to put their tackle together. Brasen, never one to keep his mouth shut, kept mimicking a vendor plying his trade to the fisherman they had joined on the Horseshoe.

The vendor, who looked like a tough, muscular older version of Chuckie Braunschweiger, pulled a red Radio Flyer wagon modified with a heavy duty, wide axle on the back to support a large stainless steel coffee urn. The vendor shouted out his menu selections of sweet rolls, coffee, sandwiches and snacks stacked orderly and neatly in the wagon. As the vendor barked out his wares, Brasen would reply to the much older and bigger man's loud sales pitch in a bold yell as to what part of the vendor's anatomy the menu items could be inserted. Gil sensed they were in trouble when the vendor turned his modified wagon into a sharp U-Turn and began pulling in earnest in their direction. Gone was the friendly sales pitch. It had been replaced by facial expressions made famous by Lon Chaney, Junior in his portrayals of the Wolf Man. Gil knew he was a goner. His eyes clicked once to the left and then to the right. Then he glanced over his right shoulder and then his left. All he saw was Lake Michigan and someone who looked like he could have been a twin of Judalyne's father bearing down on him. Brasen had his back to the vendor and was repeating his insertion directions with glee. Gil was trying to warn him, but nothing worked. Brasen didn't hear the words and didn't see the hand signs. Only when he saw the look of fear on Gil's face did his mouth stay closed. The irate concessionaire stopped behind Brasen, dropped the black handle of his food wagon, and without a word, proceeded to throw Mrs. Brasen's wire shopping cart, tackle and all, into Lake Michigan. He then looked at Gil for a moment, eyes resembling Count Dracula, and kicked Gil's tackle box into the lake saying something about what Bus had said as not being funny. The vendor actually punctuated the word *funny* more than several times with Brasen's favorite four letter word, and managed to creatively incorporate it with the various parts of speech they had learned in grammar school. Gil peered into the watery hole where his prized collection of rusted and corroded tackle had disappeared and tried to figure out how he could retrieve his treasures. The concessionaire growled something at them about their brains being made of human excrement, laughed and then picked up the black handle of his wagon, made another sweeping U-Turn, and continued shouting out the menu of his wares; this time minus Brasen's favorite instructions for anatomical insertions and four letter words.

Brasen and Gil looked at each other. Bus shrugged his shoulders and mentioned something about being lucky because, according to him, "Our asses could have been thrown in the lake along with our tackle." Bus also promised to pay Gil back for his rusted collection of hooks, sinkers, and knotted lines. Strike three had whizzed by Gil faster than his fishing tackle had submerged beneath the surface of Lake Michigan. The debt remained unpaid.

Gil had discovered depression even though he didn't know that's what he was undergoing. He wondered what else could go wrong. Summer hadn't begun officially when, two days later, his parents informed him and his three brothers that the family was moving. His first two protests echoed those of his brothers. If they moved, all of their friends would still be here and they would be a million miles away. Gil couldn't imagine life without Bus Brasen, without the guys from the neighborhood and his school mates. His protests fell on deaf ears as their mother's dream house in the suburbs was about to come true. Gil didn't see any dream. His dream had been Judalyne and he hadn't seen her since graduation day when he had given her one last look, braving a pending beating from her massive father, The Champ. He continued to question why the family had to move until his father stood up like a shot from his easy chair. That was his clue to stop questioning his mother's dream if he valued his life.

Chapter 4

Gil told Brasen about his family moving to Park Ridge, interjecting some of the same parts of speech he had heard the concessionaire use to them on the Horseshoe. Brasen asked where Park Ridge was, repeating the same parts of speech. All Gil knew was that he would be adjacent to Chicago, a little bit north and west, but light years away from their neighborhood at Belmont and Central. Gil tried objecting one more time; his last.

That's when his father set the sports section of the Herald American on his lap and explained to his oldest son that his friends were a bunch of morons. His dad's evaluation made complete sense to Gil, but they were still his friends.

It was June 15, 1951, and Gil was still moping about the coming move to Park Ridge. Feeling sorry for himself, his moping included replays of Riverview, sans vomit, the garter snake incident complete with Brasen's four letter word description and still having nocturnal emissions about Judalyne. There was also Montrose Harbor where he wondered how his fishing tackle was doing at the bottom of Lake Michigan. He also wondered about his Poppy Paul who had passed away, the mustard gas he had ingested during the war finally taking its toll on his fragile lungs. "How many strike outs could one guy have?" Gil asked himself. That's when Bus told him what he knew was an out-and-out lie and he couldn't wait to move to Park Ridge to get away from a liar.

He felt numb all over as he told Bus what he was full of.

What Bus had told him could never happen in a million, trillion years, even longer and it had to be the biggest distortion of the truth ever to come out of Brasen. But, Bus insisted he was telling the truth, explaining to Gil what he had heard on the radio. He crossed his heart several times and then mentioned what the Cubs radio announcer, Bert Wilson, had said, repeating verbatim: "Miksis'll fix us."

Gil wasn't about to believe his best pal in the whole world let alone anyone on the radio or even the Chicago Cubs. He couldn't imagine the Cubs being that stupid. Trading Andy Pafko to the Brooklyn Dodgers for Eddie Miksis; Gene Hermanski to replace him in the outfield, Bruce Edwards to catch and Joe Hatten to pitch? "No way, Brasen," he screamed at his friend. "The Cubs aren't that stupid." He paused, frustrated and added, "They're dumb, but not stupid." His mind was in a frenzy trying to picture a squatty, tubby Bruce Edwards behind the plate. He had been barely a year old when another squatty, tubby catcher named Gabby Hartnett caught for the Cubs and set all kinds of records. Edwards couldn't carry Hartnett's jock and, as far as Gil was concerned, the Dodgers needed to give up their whole team, and that wouldn't be enough, to replace Andy Pafko.

Brasen continued with the news of the trade telling him that the Cubs also gave up pitcher, Johnny Schmitz, Rube Walker and second base man, Wayne Terwilliger. That's when Gil screamed out the nastiest of nasty words because the Twig, who he thought was a good man at second, would also be a Dodger. He knew in his heart that the Cubs would be doomed to a lifetime of losing. His striking out, his being cast aside by Judalyne now became trivial in comparison. He tried to figure out a way to cancel the worst trade in the history of baseball. His history went back only thirteen years, but his collection of baseball cards and listening to Bill Stern on the radio, provided enough credence for making the trade null and void. He assumed the batting stance of his hero. His feet were square, knees bent, butt sticking out, and his right arm parallel with the ground. He swung his imaginary bat across an equally imaginary plate several times and dug in for the next pitch. There were no strike outs this time as he concentrated on driving an imaginary line drive, burying it in the pitcher's head, the imaginary pitcher being the newly acquired Joe Hatten.

He couldn't believe that Andy Pafko was a Dodger. "Not *Prushka*," he repeated, announcing his hero's nickname, the moniker given to him by Bert Wilson the Cubs radio announcer. No one heard him. He repeated his knowledge of his idol and hero to no one, expounding on Pafko's home of Boyceville, Wisconsin. Gil was lucky he knew where Wisconsin was located. He repeatedly kicked at the ground almost wearing out the toes of his official Boy Scout oxfords, totally eradicating the merit badge outline on the front soles of both shoes. Moping was the only thing he could do. Nothing else mattered. Judalyne who? He didn't care. He was still moping, more so than before, throwing a rubber ball off the front steps of his house, pretending that the steps were the Brooklyn Dodgers. Then his father came out and asked him: "How would you like to go to the Cubs game with me this afternoon?"

Gil was stunned. It was the first time his father had ever asked him to go anywhere. He stood like a zombie. "Where was the order," he wondered. His father always ordered. This was the first time ever he asked.

His father didn't wait for a response, telling his son that it would just be the two of them and then informing him that Pafko would be starting for the Dodgers. His father surprised him by proceeding to use some, but not all, of the expletives used by the concessionaire on the Horseshoe in telling his son how he felt about the trade.

Chapter 5

Father and son sat in the first row of the upper deck behind home plate. Gil had never been in the upper deck before. For that matter, he had never been with his dad alone to any place let alone Wrigley Field. Gil had been to a bunch of Cub games, most times walking into the ball park free in the late innings when the Cubs were losing and the attendance was barely into four digits. The Andy Frain ushers had always chased him, Brasen and his friends out of the box seats and strategically cut off their attempts to get to the upper deck. The seats his father had bought at the Clark Street box office were more than a treat. He couldn't wait to tell Brasen.

Maybe he had never paid much attention before, but he had never seen grass as green as he did that day. Not even at home where his father all but hand manicured their tiny lawn. The color of the infield dirt suddenly took on a different appearance. It wasn't dirt, but more like burnt gold. The lustrous green and gold was highlighted by the brilliant white of the two foul lines disappearing into the corners of left and right field. The foul lines were standing guard like sparkling white sentries for the giant curving arc of ivy, another rich, glowing green covering the outfield walls. He remembered his father's exact words as his eyes scanned the field, a look of peace and pleasure on his face that Gil had never seen before. "Ain't it somethin'," his dad reflected.

Gil agreed with his father even though it felt kind of eerie being talked to for the first time as if he were really human and not someone who was a juvenile delinquent. Could this man be the same one who yelled at him and his younger brothers? Was this the same man who could remove his belt in a blur from the loops on his khaki work pants, the scuffed brown leather at the ready, poised over his head? His brothers would never believe him if he told them about how his dad, their father, had talked and shared with him; even buying him a hot dog.

To Gil's surprise, his dad told him stories of his own baseball playing days on a semi-pro team. Gil learned that his dad even made money doing it.

"I was a submarine ball pitcher," his father had said. "I was the only southpaw on our team, the Majors S.A.C."

Then his father shocked him by saying that the initials, S.A.C. stood for sex and alcoholics club, not social and athletic club. His dad bought him a second hot dog and there was no reoccurrence of Riverview Park and the Bob's incident. There was a cup of Coca-Cola, a bag of peanuts that he seemed to eat without taking them out of their distorted shells and even a box of Cracker Jack where he gagged on the prize he ate the treat so fast. His father leaned to him and asked, "Do you know how to keep score?"

Gil thought he did. He didn't.

His father pushed a scorecard in his direction and held out a tiny wooden pencil. "Time to learn how," he said.

Before Gil realized he saw positions assigned numbers and how walks, strike outs and base runners filled in the tiny squares of the scorecard. His brothers would never believe him if he told them about how his dad, the father they both loved and feared, had given him examples of game situations and how the marks and numbers went on the card. All of this was done without a single threat and Gil was in awe at learning his father had a nickname and, even more so, how he got it. The name was Spike and Gil now knew why he feared his father.

His father got his handle when he was in a fist fight in the seventh grade. A bully tried picking on him, made the mistake of giving him a shove in the chest. The shove resulted in his father punching the bully so hard he knocked him into a wooden fence. Sticking out of the wooden fence was a rusted spike and a new name. Gil looked at his father knowing his dad, *Spike* could beat the tar out of Judalyne's father.

Gil didn't give his father his total undivided attention even though the stories were fascinating and almost too good to be true. Gil's interest was focused on the players. Not all players, mind you, and most certainly not the Cub players. White uniforms were ignored. He was looking for a Dodger player wearing number 48. Outside of Johnny Lujack of Notre Dame and his jersey number 32, there were no other numbers in his life that he cared about except perhaps 16, the legal age to get a driver's license.

His dad's attention wasn't totally on the beauty of Wrigley Field either. Father and son were both looking for the same thing. Then Gil heard his dad say something about how the ball park was his favorite place in the whole world and a state of semi-shock settled over Gil. He listened to his father share more of his private life with him. If this was a man-to-man conversation Gil felt, then it sure beat being yelled at by his father and being threatened by him to remove his vital body parts and discard them in the concrete garbage box in the alley behind their house. Not that he didn't deserve such threats, but talk about a change of pace; there wasn't a kid he knew who had ever been talked to by their parents the way his dad was actually talking to him. Parents, his father included in that group, all had graduated from the same school. He couldn't figure out what kind of school never asked questions first before sentencing students to be transferred and exiled to, of all places, a public school. Even the B.V.M. nuns who taught Gil must have had a stint in public school before being shipped off to the convent.

Gil was in awe as he listened to his father tell him how he fell in love with Wrigley Field the first time he saw it. According to his father, "It was the most beautiful place in the whole world."

Gil couldn't believe that his father was in love with a major league ball park. He began listening more intently to his father while still continuing to search for Number 48. His father continued on, stopping briefly to yell out to a vendor: "Two dogs!" The index and middle fingers of his left hand were extended in a *V* and a dollar bill was in his right. This was Gil's third hot dog and the game hadn't even started. His dad waved down another vendor and Gil had another Coke along with his dad. His dad, however, took a pass on the cotton candy.

"There's no other place in the world," his father continued then taking a sip of his Coke, "where a man could go and forget his troubles like the old ball yard." Having his dad tell him about when he was young was one of the greatest feelings Gil ever had. It was like discovering he had a brand new father. He didn't know what being philosophical was back then, but he learned. He listened to his father tell him how some people would go to the woods to find peace. His father told him about this writer, Henry David Thoreau and how he lived alone simply with nature and finding peace. His dad's father, Poppy Paul loved to fish. The closest Gil's father ever came was fishing from the piers, breakwaters and harbors along the shore of Lake Michigan; his favorite spot just north of Navy Pier. That's where Gil's rusty tackle first came from; the same rusty tackle he would never be able to use again.

"Your grandpa loved to fish," his dad said without taking his eyes off the swarm of players congregating along the third and first base lines. "He'd always drag me along to the Chain of Lakes and places like Fox Lake, Meyer's Bay, Pistakee Bay and even a tiny place called Sullivan Lake that was on the property of a private hunting club. I liked that place the best of all because we caught all kinds of fish. Your grandpa never threw a fish back no matter how small. To him it was food. When he was growing up in Prussia there were many times when he and his brothers and sisters were lucky to have something to eat."

His father took a bite of his hot dog, actually more like tearing off half the bun and stuffing it into the right side of his mouth. He took another sip of Coke, his eyes never leaving the area of the playing field. He swallowed, smacked his lips and continued. "Your grandpa took me way up to northern Wisconsin one summer for a week to a place called Eagle River." He laughed. "It seemed like a year to me. I didn't see any eagles but I did see loons and tons of hummingbirds. Now those guys were neat." Another swallow of Coke followed and then an uncharacteristic small nip at his hot dog. "The cry of the loon is still buried in my mind. And, oh, those humming-birds; what incredible little guys they were." He glanced at Gil and continued. "Remember that feeder I put up in our back-yard? Didn't see a single hummer; only a couple of sparrows and an ugly pigeon; those damned sky rats should all be buried in the City Dump."

Gil didn't like when his father started to curse. He took a sip of his Coke his own eyes scanning the players who were wearing the grey of the visiting team and asked, "Did you like being with your father?"

"Your grandfather was a tough old bird. Most times he thought he was still an officer in the Prussian Army ordering his troops around. Your grandmother was the only one who knew what he had experienced in war; the mustard gas and the bayonets; the cries and screams of the wounded; the last gasp of breath of a dying man." His father paused, glanced into the paper cup that held his Coke as if he were looking into a hypnotic pool and changed the subject. "Your Poppy Paul worked hard for every penny he got from the moment he stepped off the boat when coming to this country. He expected everyone to be the same way. And, if there was something he liked, well, everyone had to like it."

Gil listened; enamored with the details about his family he knew so little about. His father kept chatting away. Details about aunts and uncles followed; most making his dad laugh, but Gil knew better. His dad dug up more family secrets and, at first, Gil didn't notice him point towards right field. When he did, he thought he had located Andy Pafko among the cluster of grey uniforms. He hadn't. He was calling Gil's attention to a view of Lake Michigan visible over the right field bleachers. His dad began explaining to him how all kinds of people would go there to get away from their troubles and relax. He told him how Chicago's lake front was a gem and how all the people, money or not, could enjoy the beauty and not have to pay an admission. "And they didn't have to drive all the way to Eagle River to find contentment." He stopped, laughed and added, "And a slew of fish to bring home."

Then Gil told his father that he had gone fishing to Lake Michigan a couple of weeks ago with Bus Brasen. His father surprised him by laughing and telling him he knew. Brasen's mother had struck again only there was no strike from his father. His father told him he had heard all about the shopping cart getting thrown into the lake and how Brasen's parents both took turns adding lumps to their son's empty head, shifting the side where he parted his hair from the left side of his head to the right.

Then Gil, his question coming out of left field, asked: "Dad, why did Poppy Paul have to die?"

His father pondered the question, his eyes still fixed on Lake Michigan, the specks of white sails visible from their upper deck seats then said: "Gilead, there's a time to live and a time to die. It was Poppy's turn."

Gil thought, puzzled, his eyes still fixed on a handful of ball players in sparkling white uniforms gathered in left field. He asked cautiously, "Are you going to die, Dad?"

The question didn't seem to faze his father one bit. He took a sip of his Coke and looked at his son. "Gil, we're all going to die. Me, your mom, your brothers; even that knuckle head friend of yours, Bus." His dad smiled. He might beat all of us to the cemetery when his parents kill him," said his dad, the paper cup of Coke hiding most of his smile.

Then Gil felt his dad's elbow gently nudge him in the arm, and he thought he was finally going to get his comeuppance for being with Brasen and losing his fishing tackle. Instead, his father pointed and said the magic words: "There he is."

Gil didn't see him at first and he must have asked his dad forty eight times in three seconds to point him out. Then he saw his hero, his magnificent numerals adorning the back of the grey traveling uniform of the enemy, the white *B* on his cap; the detested Dodger blue. He stuffed the remaining half of his hot dog into his mouth forgetting all about Riverview and Judalyne and began to wave. Then Gil called out his name, a first name recognition reserved for the closest of idols. "Andy!" he yelled out almost choking on the mouth full of semi-chewed bun, meat and mustard. Gil was the only one who could even recognize the name that came out. His father jammed the remainder of his hot dog in his mouth, stood up joining his son, his own hot dog sticking out of his mouth like a giant cigar. He was waving, but knew that shouting wouldn't work. They waved, chewed and swallowed until they could at least get Pafko's first name out where it could be understood. They repeated, Andy at the top of their voices over and over, but he never looked up.

When the Cubs took the field Gil and his dad booed. All of Wrigley Field booed. Even the ghosts of seasons past booed. They booed the Dodger batters. After all, they were from Brooklyn and they were always winning while the Cubs were always waiting until next year. Then, Andy Pafko entered the on deck circle swinging several bats. An epidemic of cheers spread through the stands. When he stepped into the batter's box, scooping up a handful of dirt, rubbing his palms together, the crowd noise grew. Then Pat Piper announced his name over the public address system and the people in Brooklyn could hear the crowd even without the radio. Gil couldn't hear his own cheers. The fans were on their feet, watching, as if for the last time, the classic stance of a master. Gil's eyes were glued to his shiny Louisville Slugger bat being leveled over the plate with several quick practice swings. He yelled for him to hit it out of the park so loud, so many times, he thought his head would explode. Then his hero heard him. There was the windup and then the glistening white ball hurling towards the plate only to be met by the blur of the bat, the sunshine creating a blinding glare. There was an awesome crack and the ball was launched into a high trajectory over the Cub team, their heads turning, eyes knowing, watching as the ball found its way easily into the left field bleachers. There was hysteria. There was pandemonium. Gil was standing and found himself jumping so high he almost went over the railing of the upper deck. He and his dad cheered, yelled, clapped and hugged and didn't stop until the familiar figure had circled the bases and vanished into the dugout along the first base line. After his hero's homer Gil was convinced, and told his father, that the Cubs would see the terrible mistake they had made and call off the trade. His father agreed with him about the dreadful error the Cub's management had made, using language that didn't shock his son because he had heard it all before at home. It felt kind of good that he wasn't on the receiving end of his dad's words, many of which had been banned in their house by his mother, and that the Chicago Cubs were getting an ear full. His father's questioning of their mentality, the legality of their combined births, and that each had a canine relative on a branch of their family trees had certainly made its way into the broadcast booth up and behind them. The entire listening audience would surely descend upon the Chicago Cubs organization with threats, including bodily harm, if Andy wasn't back in a Cub uniform for the next game. He wasn't and the fans made it known to the Cubs management about the trade organizing the first boycott of a major league baseball team in the history of the game. It didn't matter that Bruce Edwards, the new Cub catcher, also hit a homer, his portly torso lumbering around the bases in contrast to the gazelle like strides of Gil's hero. He was convinced that Andy Pafko would be back in center field where he was born to enhance the ivy, set records and thrill the fans by throwing out base runners that were foolish enough to test his mighty arm.

His father agreed with much of what he had said as they drove home in the family Hudson. The wind was whistling through a gash in the driver side door where his father had clipped their fence backing into the garage one night coming home from a party. His mother had claimed that his father had, in her words, "One too many," and was doing at least the speed of sound when the accident happened. His dad had denied it. There wasn't any denying how Gil loved talking with his dad that day.

One other day stuck in his mind; that was the time when the baseball season was over for the Cubs. The Cub season officially ended just after the All-Star game, but not for Pafko and the Dodgers. They were in the midst of a pennant hunt. He had convinced his parents to let him go to high school with Brasen and the guys. "Dad," he started out his plea without going to his knees, "I know we're going to move to Park Ridge and that's far away, but it's on your way to work. You could drop me off. Then I could wait after school for you to pick me up. I could get all my homework done. Heck, Dad, I think I could make the honor roll. Honest."

Gil's quasi-victory was the last of their father-son talks.

Gil and his dad never got back to see the Cubs play after Andy Pafko had been traded and he had learned the real reason for going to Wrigley Field. His father died suddenly that September with the Cub management planning for next year and Gil three weeks into high school. His father had been in the garage trying to fix the gash in the car door before winter set in and had a heart attack. Life, as Gil knew it, stopped as it did for his mother who never did get to move into her dream house in Park Ridge.

Years later, after that depressing summer of 1951, Gil was comfortable being called, Gilead. He was married and the father of three daughters. His daughters followed right in a row and he originally referred to them as Strikes One, Two, and Three because they were all born during successive baseball seasons, one in late April, another in May, and another in June; June 15th to be exact. The nicknames were quickly and quietly changed without fanfare to Peanuts, Dim-Dom, and Bingo, nicknames of several of his Cub heroes. He even had a nickname for his wife, calling her Pru, a shortened version of, Prushka. Strikes one through three became a private thing between daughters and their father as he tried to stop being like his dad on the one hand and more like the new dad he had discovered that day at Wrigley Field. Each year when one of the girls would turn thirteen, the age he was when he and his father saw the Cubs and Dodgers play, he would take the birthday girl to a Cub game as her one-on-one present from him. Weather and schedule permitting, he would drive the daughter designate into the city from their house, ironically, in Park Ridge, in the family Oldsmobile. There was no breeze blowing through a rusted gash in the driver side door. Rust was a taboo because it reminded him of how many of the Cub teams played throughout the years. He'd park the Oldsmobile on a side street several miles from the ball park and take her on the Addison Street bus the way he used to with Brasen and the guys when they were a lot younger than thirteen and striking terror in the hearts of the Andy Frain ushers patrolling Wrigley Field.

It was never possible to get the same seats he and his dad had, but he would point out to whichever daughter was being treated where her grandfather and he had sat. The particular birthday girl would listen, a Cub hat snug on her head, a scorecard and program book in her lap and a Coca-Cola and hot dog oozing mustard filling her hands as she listened about a man she had only seen in snap shots; the man who had taught her father how to keep score of a baseball game.

None of the girls ever complained about going to a baseball game and hearing stories about their grandfather and their father's other hero, their great grandfather; a man known as Poppy Paul. Instead, they hid their excitement and curiosity as only thirteen year old girls can do on a trip to Wrigley Field. Then, after seeing pictures of several ball players in the program book who bordered on the handsome side, their enthusiasm became less camouflaged as they nonchalantly dog eared certain pages for later reference.

After the youngest, *Bingo*, had her birthday treat, Gilead began taking the entire family to a game. It cost him close to the national debt. However, as he looked around Wrigley Field, unable to see Lake Michigan from where they were sitting in the grandstand, he could picture the look on his father's face as his eyes drank in the green grass of the field, the deep, lush ivy covering the curved outfield wall from brilliant white foul line to brilliant white foul line, and the golden dirt of the infield. He could hear his father's words about the old ball yard and he was thirteen again. There was his dad and *Prushka*. There was Brasen with the guys and even Judalyne who he would still see in a quick glance every year or so pulling out the curled graduation class picture from a cardboard box in their basement. There were his Poppy Paul's words of wisdom making his heart glow and his smile being hidden by a cup of Coke. What had been the worst year of his life somehow had become the best and he never forgot it; never forgot his idols, especially Prushka; then, years later hearing the news that his idol had been given his last at bat before rounding the bases for Heaven.

Title: Where Have All the Go-Go's Gone?

Part I

- Author: Richard Baran
- Publisher: TotalRecall Publications, Inc.
- Hard Cover, ISBN: 9781590952399
- Paperback, ISBN: 9781590952405
- Ebook, Nook, Kindle, ISBN: 9781590952412
- Number of pages: 304
- Publication Date: 2015

Bo Pepperwall's intelligence dwarfed Mensa's parameters. He was perceived as strange thereby resulting in his being ridiculed by many, shunned by most and being called, Bo the Schmoe by all. Then he faced a dilemma. He had to choose between money (which he never had) and morals (which he also lacked). Should he weasel a part of his recently widowed sister's inheritance for a business venture or should he turn in the killer of her husband, his despicable brother-in-law? He chooses both. Bo opens La Tinkerbelle's a Go-Go, a 1960's retro discotheque in an abandoned factory building in a Chicago slum using a theme from the legend of Peter Pan. Surrounding himself with bizarre employees (each having a unique vision of reality) who put fun into dysfunctional, his dream nearly goes bust. Then a Chicago gossip columnist prints a story that has customers lined up and Bo collides with his dilemma. The collision buries him in money and public adulation. Success, however, can't cover his moral guilt in the surprise ending to this murder mystery farce that is more farce than mystery.

Title: When Will They Ever Learn?

Part II Where Have All the Go-Go's Gone?
- Author: Richard Baran
- Publisher: TotalRecall Publications, Inc.
- Hard Cover, ISBN: 9781590952429
- Paperback, ISBN: 9781590952436
- Ebook, Nook, Kindle, ISBN: 9781590952443
- Number of pages: 220
- Publication Date: 2015

Bo Pepperwall, a card carrying member of Mensa, dreamer, conniver and ridiculed lifelong loser opens *La Tinkerbelle's a Go-Go.* A 1960's retro discotheque located in a Chicago slum, he uses a theme from the legend of Peter Pan that includes a scantily clad Tinker Bell. He finances his business by weaseling part of his sister's inheritance away from her. He also witnesses the murder of his despicable brother-in-law, the mayor of Glen Forest on the Watercourse, a prestigious Chicago North Shore community. Bo, however, remains a loser and his garish disco faces bankruptcy until an article by a Chicago gossip columnist turns it into a bonanza. That same day, Tinker Bell's outraged mother accidentally sets fire to La Tinkerbelle's and destroys the booming business. Bo and his employees—along with two black cats named Heckle and Jeckle—end up in court charged with violations of the Mann Act; contributing to the delinquency of minors; ignoring EPA laws; cruelty to animals and presenting lewd and indecent performances. Bo turns in the killer and the court finds him innocent of the criminal charges in the surprise ending to this murder mystery zany comedy.

Title: The Jacket

- Author: Richard Baran
- Publisher: TotalRecall Publications, Inc.
- Hard Cover ISBN: 9781590955659
- Paperback, ISBN: 9781590955666
- Ebook, Nook, Kindle, ISBN: 9781590955673
- Number of pages: 352
- Publication Date: 2013

Tidge Mackiewicz, new patriarch of his family, received several orders from his dying father, Kid Scream. One order stated that Tidge should quit believing in Santa Claus and stop acting like every day was Christmas. Tidge should also abandon his belief that the Luftwaffe shot down Santa Claus on Christmas Eve in 1944 and Santa survived.

Title: The Dutchman's Gift

- Author: Richard Baran
- Publisher: TotalRecall Publications, Inc.
- Paperback, ISBN: 9781590952979
- Ebook, Nook, Kindle, ISBN: 9781590952986
- Number of pages: 124
- Publication Date: 2015

A twelve year old boy finds a magical Apache arrowhead while hiking with his grandfather in the Superstition Mountains of Arizona. The arrowhead transports the boy from a Disney World rollercoaster ride back over one hundred and fifty years to the Superstitions where he meets "The Lost Dutchman."

Title: Shutter Bug

- Author: Richard Baran
- Publisher: TotalRecall Publications, Inc.
- Paperback, ISBN: 9781590953167
- Ebook, Nook, Kindle, ISBN: 9781590953174
- Number of pages: 176
- Publication Date: 2016

Emma Grace Waveland, a self-proclaimed Shutter Bug at twelve, finds herself transported from a safari in Disney World to Africa's Serengeti where she joins a group of professional hunters who capture wild animals for zoos. Her new adventure brings her face-to-face with deadly crocodiles, a giant rhino, a python, a lady photographer who looks like a young version of her great grandmother, hunters who resemble old movie stars and a camp cook with mysterious powers. Her family doesn't believe her when she returns from her trip, but she has evidence on her cameras' memory cards and her iPhone.

**A Mouse Gate Adventure
Book What's your adventure?**

www.mousegate.com

9 781590 953181